D0899720

Revealing

the

Dragons

(Stonefire Dragons #3)

Jessie Donovan

This book is a work of fiction. Names, characters, places, and incidents are either the product of the writer's imagination or are used fictitiously, and any resemblance to actual persons, living or dead, business establishments, events, or locales is entirely coincidental.

Revealing the Dragons
Copyright © 2015 Laura Hoak-Kagey
Mythical Lake Press, LLC
First Print Edition

Cover Art by Clarissa Yeo of Yocla Designs.

ISBN 13: 978-1942211174

To anyone who has ever tried to make a difference in the world

Thank you!

Other Books by Jessie Donovan

Stonefire Dragons
Sacrificed to the Dragon
Seducing the Dragon
Revealing the Dragons
Healed by the Dragon
Reawakening the Dragon
Loved by the Dragon
Surrendering to the Dragon
Cured by the Dragon

Lochguard Highland Dragons
The Dragon's Dilemma
The Dragon Guardian
The Dragon's Heart
The Dragon Warrior (Feb 2017)

Asylums for Magical Threats
Blaze of Secrets
Frozen Desires
Shadow of Temptation
Flare of Promise

Cascade Shifters
Convincing the Cougar
Reclaiming the Wolf
Cougar's First Christmas
Resisting the Cougar

CHAPTER ONE

Melanie Hall-MacLeod brushed the cheek of her five-month-old daughter, Annabel, one more time before looking up at her sister-in-law and saying, "Remember, she'll only go to sleep if she has her stuffed green dinosaur. And Jack needs his baby blankie."

Her sister-in-law, Arabella MacLeod, raised an eyebrow, which also raised the scar near her temple. "Have you temporarily forgotten the last five months? You know, when I was here at least three times a week helping out with the twins?"

Before Mel could reply, the third woman standing near the door, Evie Marshall, interjected, "Give her a break, Arabella. This is the first time she'll be away from her babies for an entire night."

Ara replied, "Yours and Bram's cottage is a five-minute walk from here. We could probably hear Tristan if he shouted."

Melanie was about to set them straight when she felt Tristan's presence at her back before he rubbed up and down her arms. His touch soothed some of her tension and she leaned back against his muscled chest. His arms went around her and she let out a sigh. The world could be ending and Tristan's touch would still ease her worries.

His deep voice rumbled, "If you two have everything you need, then maybe you should go."

Evie raised an eyebrow. "You are aware that we're watching your children for free, right?"

Tristan said, "And?"

Evie shook her head and Melanie jumped in, "Ignore him. We're extremely grateful for you two volunteering to watch Jack and Annabel. I've spent every moment either taking care of them or finishing my book. A night off, despite my mother-half worrying, will hopefully refresh me for the shit storm to come after the book releases next week."

Evie tilted her head. "I don't know if it'll be that bad, Mel. After all, the reception of the article about mine and Bram's mating ceremony went well. Not one attack, and if anything, more people are 'dragon watching' more than ever before, hoping to catch a glimpse of a flying dragon."

Mel leaned more against her mate's chest. "A mating ceremony is one thing, but a book humanizing, for lack of a better word, the dragon-shifters is another. Doing that might push for equality, which many most definitely don't want. Permanent change can be scary, especially if it involves giant dragons maybe moving into your neighborhood."

Evie adjusted the sleeping Jack in her arms. "Nothing you're doing is breaking the law. Besides, even if people become upset, you're safe here. Bram would never allow anything to happen to you." Tristan grunted and Evie rolled her eyes. "Or, I should say, Tristan won't allow anything to happen to you."

Mel sighed. "I know, but what happens if it fails? I'd one day like my children to be able to see their grandparents and uncle."

Tristan squeezed her gently and said, "Soon, my little human. We'll find a way."

"I hope so," Mel whispered. She'd been on Stonefire's land for a little over a year. While phone calls and video chats helped, she missed her parents and younger brother so much it hurt.

Evie gave her a sympathetic look before straightening her shoulders. "Right, then, Arabella. Let's leave the two lovebirds alone. I'm sure they have lots of catching up to do."

Tristan said, "Yes, so only call if it's an emergency. I plan to keep Melanie very, very busy."

She elbowed her mate. "My definition of an emergency and Tristan's vary. His involves blood and dying. Mine includes things like high fevers and uncontrollable crying. Call if you need anything."

Arabella finally spoke up again. "If we don't know how to handle something, Bram will." Ara looked to Evie. "Let's go before Melanie thinks of another reason to keep us here."

Evie nodded. As the human woman and the dragonwoman walked away, Mel shouted, "Thank you! Remember to call!"

Evie raised a hand in acknowledgment. Soon, the two women disappeared behind a cottage.

She sighed. "I hope everything goes okay."

"It will."

Tristan walked them back a step inside their cottage and shut the door. Melanie turned in his arms. "You checked your phone, right? It's fully charged?"

Tristan raised a hand to her cheek and brushed her skin with his fingers. "Yes, love. Fully charged, although Bram knows what he's doing."

She placed a hand on Tristan's chest. "It's just, with Jack and Annabel gone, it feels like a part of me left with them."

One corner of Tristan's mouth ticked up. "If you're like this now, what are you going to do when they're old enough to live on their own?"

Swatting his chest, she frowned. "That's a surefire way to ease my worry. You're the worst, Tristan MacLeod."

He chuckled. "And yet you're the one who agreed to be my mate."

His gaze turned heated and Mel's heart rate kicked up. "You have your moments."

Leaning down, Tristan brushed his cheek against hers. "Then I'll make sure this is one of them."

As one of his hands rubbed down her back and rested on her ass, heat spread through her body. "You're not even going to try to woo me first?"

He massaged her bum. The feel of his warm, strong hands molding and sculpting her flesh sent a jolt between her legs. With each squeeze, it became harder for Mel to stand upright.

Even after being mated a year, all her dragonman had to do was touch her and she turned wet and needy. Not that she would ever give in easily to him.

With a husky voice, he said, "Who needs words when I can do this?"

He nibbled her earlobe and she leaned against his chest for support. Then he kissed his way down her neck until he bit where her shoulder met her neck. As he soothed the bite with his tongue, Melanie whispered, "I love our children and can't imagine life without them, but I've missed not having to squeeze in sex in between feedings or naps."

Tristan moved so he could look into her eyes. "Me too, love. However, our twins are in the hands of capable people and I have the whole night with you to myself."

Revealing the Dragons

She batted her eyelashes. "And what in the world should we do? Maybe clean the kitchen? Or catch up on laundry?"

Her mate growled and hauled her body against his. His hard cock poked her stomach through his trousers. "Forget the bloody cleaning. My plans include devouring you properly."

Her pussy pulsed as memories of Tristan lapping between her legs filled her mind. "Then, dragonman, you'd better get started. After all, we only have twelve hours before Evie and Ara bring the twins home."

"I think learning to function on little sleep will work to our advantage tonight."

She laughed. "Just make sure to feed me once in a while or I will get cranky. Not even your hot dragon self will be safe."

He nuzzled her cheek. "Soon you won't be able to say anything but my name. I think I'll be fine."

She opened her mouth to reply but then Tristan kissed her. As his tongue stroked hers, Melanie decided words could wait.

~~~

As Tristan explored the inside of his mate's mouth, his dragon growled. *Why are you waiting? It's been too long. Fuck her now. She likes it hard.*

Shut it, or I won't give you a turn.

His inner beast hissed. *You can't deny me. I am stronger.*

Last warning.

As his dragon sulked and retreated, Tristan hugged Melanie tighter. The way her soft stomach cushioned his cock made him even harder.

11

He broke the kiss and ran a finger under the band of her jeans, loving the softness of her skin. "Take these off or I rip them off."

Melanie raised an eyebrow. "At the rate you rip off my clothes, I soon won't have anything to wear."

He undid the top button and slowly unzipped her jeans. "Then wear skirts with nothing underneath. I like easy access."

"I need some barriers between me and your cock. Taking care of twins is exhausting and as much as I love you, there are moments when I don't want anyone to touch me."

Tristan stilled. "You've never mentioned this before."

Melanie shrugged one shoulder. "I didn't want to risk your dragon getting out of control due to lack of sex."

His dragon huffed. *I can refrain sometimes. She only needs to ask.*

Cupping her face, he ordered, "If you ever need a break, tell me. I can't take care of you if I don't know what you need."

His mate smiled. "Oh, Tristan. You can be sweet when you try."

He grunted. "Don't go ruining my reputation now."

Melanie laughed and some of his tension eased. As much of a bastard it might make him, he very much wanted to fuck his mate senseless as soon as he could get her naked.

When she ran a hand up his chest and around his neck, she played with the hairs at the back of his head; his hope soared higher.

Mel's husky voice caressed his ears. "Let me be very clear about tonight. I want you both on top of me and in me, dragonman, so hurry up and fuck me."

Without another word, Tristan pulled his mate close and thrust his tongue between her lips. As he stroked the inside of her hot, silky mouth, she dug her nails into his scalp. His dragon chimed in. *She is willing. Take her now.*

Picking her up, Mel wrapped her legs around his waist, never pausing the strokes of her tongue against his. With a growl, Tristan walked them to the living area and perched his mate on the back of the couch. He ran his hands to her thighs and gently pushed. She opened without hesitation.

She wants us. Hurry.

Even after a year of being mated, his dragon hadn't grown any less attached to their human.

He pulled away long enough to bark, "Put your hands on my shoulders and lift your arse."

Melanie complied. He tugged her jeans until they were off and he tossed them aside. Slowly, he rubbed his hands up her calves, paused to brush the underside of her knee, and then rubbed slow circles up the insides of her thighs. By the time he traced the edge of her panties with his forefinger, her breathing was fast and he could smell how wet she was for him.

His dragon hissed. *For us. She wants both of us.*

Ignoring his dragon, Tristan ran a finger through her swollen flesh and Melanie moaned. When he lightly scraped her clit, his mate whispered, "Rip off the damn panties and fuck me already."

He tore off the black material and leaned down to place a kiss on his mate's lips as he continued to trace her pussy lips with his forefinger. "I'm just making sure you're nice and ready for me, because once I start, I won't be able to stop."

"We have eleven hours and fifty minutes left. Stop wasting time, Tristan. Of course I'm wet and ready for you."

He growled, "I love you," before thrusting a finger inside her pussy. Melanie tossed back her head and moved on his finger.

13

Fuck. She was already dripping down his hand.

He removed his finger and Melanie let out a sound of protest. "Stop playing with me, dragonman. I want an orgasm, and I want it now."

The corner of his mouth ticked up. "So impatient, my little human."

She raised an eyebrow. "Two can play dirty."

Melanie placed her hands on her breasts and squeezed. He wanted to suck her nipples hard, but they were currently off-limits because of their soreness from breastfeeding. His mate was taunting him.

Shucking his trousers and boxer shorts, Tristan placed his hands on her inner thighs and pressed her legs wider. Then he traced her slit with the head of his cock, careful never to touch her clit. Melanie wiggled to try to get the contact she craved, but Tristan moved out of the way.

She frowned. "Fine, you've made your point. We'll call it a draw if it means you'll put your cock where it belongs."

"Belongs?"

A year ago, Mel would've blushed and hesitated to reply. After a year, however, she merely brushed the outside of her pussy as she said, "Here, Tristan. Your cock belongs to me."

The sight made him release a drop of pre-cum.

His dragon roared. *Fuck her. Now.*

Not needing any encouragement, he entered in one swift thrust. Mel grabbed his shoulders and moaned. "Yes, now take me hard and make me scream."

Grabbing her hips, he positioned her a little more toward him before he moved. As he pistoned his lower body hard enough for his balls to slap against the back of her arse, he never broke eye contact. He loved watching a flush creep up his mate's cheeks as she moaned louder.

He adjusted the angle of her hips and his mate whispered, "Yes, right there. I'm so close, Tristan."

"Hold tight to my shoulders."

She nodded and he moved one hand between her legs to brush her clit. Mel murmured, "Harder."

He pressed against her hard bud and Mel dug her nails into his back. As she scraped them down to his waist, he relaxed the pressure of his finger.

Mel growled. "Keep this up, and I'm going to provoke your dragon to fuck me instead."

His inner beast preened. *See? She wants me. I will take over.*

No bloody way.

Tristan pulled out his cock slowly, before slamming into Mel's pussy. Her nails once more dug into his skin and he murmured, "Your threats mean I'll just own your pussy that much slower."

He repeated the action and Mel hissed. "I'm going to remember this for later. The next time you ask me to suck your cock, I'm going to draw it out until you beg."

An image of his mate licking his cock in slow, deliberate motions made his balls tighten. "If this is all it takes for that kind of torture, then prepare yourself, love."

Slowly, he circled in and out of Mel, casually brushing her clit with each thrust.

When she clenched around him on purpose, it took everything he had to keep from coming, but the combined flush and light sheen of sweat on his mate's skin made both man and beast satisfied.

JESSIE DONOVAN

He only wished she were naked. He wanted to caress every inch of her skin.

"Tristan, please."

Lowering his head, he kissed her. As her moans vibrated against his lips, he increased the pressure against her clit. He broke their kiss long enough to whisper, "Come for me, love."

Rubbing her clit hard, in a circular motion, she screamed.

Her pussy clenched and released his cock. Taking hold of her hips with both hands again, he moved faster. The pressure built at the base of his spine.

He was ready to brand his mate with his scent.

His dragon managed to get out, *Yes, brand her. Then it's my turn.*

Rather than argue, Tristan kissed his mate again. The combination of her taste and her hot grip on his cock was enough to push him over the edge.

Tristan growled and stilled inside his mate as his orgasm hit him. Each spurt from his dick sent his mate into orgasm again.

He deepened his kiss, stroking and dominating her mouth. She would have no doubt that she belonged to him.

Once she'd wrung the last drop from his cock, he pulled her close to rub her back as she came down from her multiple orgasms. The way she leaned against him for support stoked his ego.

Our mate is sated but she can take more. It's my turn.

Ignoring his dragon, he kissed the top of Mel's head. "You screamed, but I don't think it was loud enough."

"Oh, really?"

He leaned back to stare into his mate's beautiful green eyes. The sated look made his dragon hum. *Is it my turn yet? I will make her scream louder.*

He brushed the soft skin at his mate's hip. "Should I try a bit harder?"

She smiled as she traced shapes on his chest with a finger. "Only if you're naked, first. I don't like this shirt getting in the way."

He ran a hand from her hip to under her top and caressed her round belly. "Only if I can lick every inch of your sexy body first."

Some of her confidence faded. "I'm not quite as sexy as I once was, I'm afraid."

He growled. "Nonsense." Lifting the hem of her top, he exposed her belly and traced the stretch marks left from her pregnancy. "These are battle scars you should wear proudly."

He pulled out before leaning down and kissing each mark in turn. Once finished, he stood again and placed a hand on his mate's face.

As Tristan stroked her cheek, Melanie's eyes grew wet. "There's that sweetness again. Although, given it was two of your children, they are more like war wounds."

"Whatever they are, you're sexier to me now than ever before, so strip, human, so I can make you scream louder."

And for once, Melanie didn't fight or tease him. She merely took off her clothes.

As she stripped to reveal her gorgeous curves, Tristan was reminded how lucky he was to have Mel as his mate. He would do anything to protect her.

Turning around, his mate faced him and crossed her arms over her breasts. She gave him a deliberate once-over. "Well? Why do you still have your clothes on? You're behind."

Tristan pulled his top over his head and rushed to his female. Scooping her up, he nuzzled her neck; her scent a drug he would never have enough of. "Not yet, but that's where I plan to be in about ten seconds."

Melanie laughed and Tristan carried his mate to their bedroom. It was time to let his dragon-half out and make her scream.

CHAPTER TWO

One Week Later

Tristan tapped his finger against the arm of the chair. When his clan leader, Bram, finally hung up the phone, Tristan asked, "Why am I here? I'd rather be with my mate today."

Bram raised an eyebrow. "As I would rather be with mine. But do I ever call you to my cottage without a reason?"

"No, but whatever you need to say, just say it."

Bram shook his head. "If you weren't my friend of thirty years, Tristan, I would actually try to instill some manners into you." Tristan merely shrugged and his clan leader continued. "Right, the reason I called you in here is to give you the coordinates of a safe location to stash your family in case the worst happens. We have no idea what response the general public will have to the release of Melanie's book today and I want to play it safe."

"Then why did you wait so long to tell me this? You've known for months when the book would come out."

Bram crossed his arms over his chest. "Given the recent trouble of traitors in the clan over the last year, I thought you'd understand my need to be cautious."

Tristan's dragon piped in. *We trust him. Don't be so rude. He wants to help protect our mate.*

Ignoring his inner beast, Tristan replied, "Then hurry up and tell me what I need to know, Bram. When I left, Mel was pacing and muttering to herself. Even with Arabella and Evie there, she needs me."

Bram uncrossed his arms, picked up a folder on his desk, and held it out. Tristan took it as his friend explained, "Finlay Stewart has graciously offered us protection on the Isle of Skye for you and your family, if we need it. The location is remote enough to protect you. Not only that, there are numerous caves and cottages listed for you to choose from. If things turn violent and humans threaten Mel's life, I want you to take her to one of those locations."

Tristan looked up. "The last time you took someone to a safe location, it was compromised. How do we know this time will be any different? After all, the dragon hunters are currently a major pain in our arses."

"This time, we know they are around and dangerous. Not only that, but Protectors from both Stonefire and Lochguard will be located around the island to act as lookouts and help if needed."

"You're trusting the Scottish bastard a lot considering the alliance is a mere four months old."

Bram gave him a piercing blue-eyed stare. "He saved my mate's life. I'm not sure what else he could do to prove his sincerity and dedication to the alliance."

Tristan grunted. "But why Skye? Lewis or any of the Western Isles would be more remote."

"Transporting five-month-old twins is quite a process. Skye is a bit easier to manage. Besides, from what I hear, the residents of Skye have a history of helping the dragon-shifters and garnering their help in return."

Revealing the Dragons

Skye is remote enough and closer to the Scottish dragon clan. It is a good choice, his dragon said.

Since when are you a master of geography?

You are a teacher. Your knowledge is my knowledge. I pay attention when you instruct the young ones on where it's safe to fly.

Rather than admit his dragon had a point, Tristan focused back on Bram. "And the transport details?"

"It will be by dragonflight. Dr. Sid devised carry cases for the twins to protect them from the cold." Bram motioned toward the folder in Tristan's hands. "The rest of the details are in there. Read them over, discuss them with Mel, and then get back to me and Kai. Since reading a three-hundred page book will take some time, I don't expect anything to happen today. Still, read it and discuss it with your mate as soon as possible."

Bram's tone brooked no argument. "Right, then can I go? Mel hasn't slept well in days and my dragon is not happy about it."

His clan leader waved a hand. "Go. I'll send someone over when the shipment of her books arrives here later today."

With a grunt, Tristan left Bram's cottage and headed home. As much as he appreciated his friend's precaution, Tristan knew there was no bloody way Mel would leave the clan. He only hoped there wasn't any violence as a result of her book, because then the real test would begin—a battle between his dragon's need to protect and the need to support his mate and stand by her side when she needed it most.

~~~

Melanie paced the length of her living room, down the hall to the door, and back again. Where was Tristan?

21

Without him by her side to calm her or keep her grounded, a million thoughts raced through her head.

Maybe everyone who bought her book would simply return it. Or, if they kept the book, then maybe a plane would appear out of nowhere to drop bombs on Stonefire, killing everyone she held dear.

Tristan would say she was crazy, but an exposé of the dragon-shifters had never been released before; there was no way to judge how the public would respond.

Not even holding one of her babies would help calm her mind. She needed the solid strength and bluntness of her mate.

Once she reached the living area again, Arabella looked up from her laptop. "Your pacing is distracting. Can't you go clean the kitchen or something so I can finish my work?"

She stopped in front of her sister-in-law and glared. "You came here of your own desire. I didn't ask you to come, let alone bring one of your laptops here to work on. You can leave if it's that much of a bother."

Evie, who was sitting on the floor and building a tower of blocks with little Murray, frowned and chimed in, "You don't need to bite her head off, Melanie. We're here for support, especially since Bram needed to talk with Tristan."

Melanie paced around the living area. "I don't understand why Bram couldn't come here, or do a teleconference."

Evie scrutinized her. "You're definitely not yourself today. The Melanie Hall-MacLeod I know goes out of her way to make things easy for everyone but herself. You're stressed, love. Either share your thoughts or I'll force some chamomile tea down your throat since Bram would frown upon me using a sedative."

Mel blinked. "You want to drug me?"

REVEALING THE DRAGONS

Arabella chuckled, which only made Mel blink again. Ara closed her laptop and crossed her arms over her chest. "Even I'm tempted to give you a sleep aid of some sort. You're driving everyone crazy, Melanie, especially since there's nothing to do but wait and see how things go."

Mel sighed. "I know that, but it doesn't make it any easier. Especially since I couldn't find a publisher who would publish my book so I had to do it myself."

Ara shook her head. "You had twenty thousand pre-orders for the ebook version alone. I'd say you did well enough by publishing it yourself and it won't be long before every book shop in the country wants to stock *Revealing the Dragons: the Day-to-Day Lives of a British Dragon-Shifter Clan.*"

Evie squeaked a toy dragon at Murray before scrunching her nose. "I still say you should've picked a shorter, snazzier title. It almost sounds...academic, which usually means boring."

Mel huffed. "It's supposed to sound academic. I wasn't about to write a tabloid tell-all." Evie smiled and Mel understood. "You were trying to rile me up, weren't you?"

Evie shrugged. "It's better than you pacing until you wear a hole in the carpet."

After living so long with Tristan, it took everything Mel had not to growl. "Yes, but get me too riled up and I'll wake the twins. You'll find out soon enough what it's like to have two young children to care for and how precious it is when they take a nap."

Evie's eyes turned wistful. "I can't wait." Then her friend's gaze turned devious. "Besides, Bram can take care of Murray during the day, for the most part, if I need him to."

Mel sighed. "You understand he's the clan leader, right, Evie? And he may, I don't know, have things to do?" Ara snickered and Mel turned her gaze on her sister-in-law. "Are we entertaining you, sister?"

Arabella nodded. "You two are better than most human TV shows I watch. By all means, keep going."

Melanie was about to switch the focus of her extra energy on Arabella when the front door opened and Tristan's voice sounded down the hallway. "Melanie?"

"Tristan." She rushed down the hallway and engulfed her mate in her arms. "Please tell me Bram didn't have bad news."

As her mate's hand rubbed her back, she melted against him. His voice rumbled under her ear. "No, not bad news. It was just Bram being Bram."

She pulled back and looked up at her mate. "That isn't very helpful."

Evie's voice came from behind her. "He means Bram has a back-up plan, in case things go wrong."

She swung her head at her friend, who was no doubt holding Murray as a form of protection to keep her from scolding too harshly. Mel's brows came together. "You knew and didn't tell me?"

Evie shrugged. "Bram is clan leader, which nearly makes me one as well since I'm his other half. I can't share his secrets without his permission."

Tristan rubbed her back a little harder. "She's right, love."

Under normal circumstances, Mel knew Evie had information she couldn't share. Yet her book's release day was the culmination of nearly a year's worth of work and Mel didn't like being left in the dark.

She looked back up to Tristan's brown eyes. "What is this back-up plan, then?"

"You aren't going to like it."

She slapped his chest. "Tell me."

Tristan held up a folder in his free hand. "Inside is a list of safe places to flee on the Isle of Skye if we need it."

Mel frowned. "Scotland? He trusts Finn that much?"

Tristan nodded. "Apparently so. Although, the real question is if things turn sour, would you even go?"

She stared into her mate's eyes. They were full of curiosity and a touch of concern. "If it were up to you, we'd leave right now."

Tristan rubbed smaller circles on her back. "Yes, but it's not solely up to me. I promised you I would always try to ask first, so I'm asking."

Not caring that she had an audience, Mel whispered, "I love you, Tristan MacLeod."

He smiled. "That still doesn't give me an answer, my little human. Would you go?"

"No, I don't think I could." Evie made a sound of protest and Mel looked over at her friend. "It's my work that's putting everyone in danger. It's taken me a year to gain the acceptance of most of the clan. What do you think would happen if I brought a heap of danger to Stonefire and then fled?"

Evie's face turned grim. "They would hate you more than ever before. Maybe even think you did it on purpose, to make them suffer."

Tristan growled. "Anyone who would think that is an idiot. My mate hasn't hurt anyone, ever. She's too big-hearted."

Mel smiled up at her mate. "Thanks for the support." She looked back to Evie. "If it truly turns into an all-out battle, I'll send the children away to safety. But my place is here with the clan. I have too many interviews lined up over the next few days that might help stem any acts of violence."

Evie shook her head. "You have more faith in the media than I do."

Mel snuggled into her mate's chest. "To change the laws, we need the media on our side. So yes, I am optimistic because otherwise, I might be risking everyone's safety for nothing."

Evie readjusted Murray on her hip. "Right, then we'll all try extra hard. Do you need to go over your talking points again?"

Before Mel could reply, Tristan squeezed her and said, "You need a rest, Melanie Hall-MacLeod. Did you eat breakfast while I was with Bram?"

Turning her head into Tristan's chest, she mumbled, "No."

Her dragonman growled. "I'm feeding you and then you're taking a nap."

Mel looked up. "What about Jack and Annabel?"

Tristan looked past her to Evie. "I'm sure you and Arabella can manage."

Arabella's voice carried from the living area. "You could ask me, brother."

Tristan dropped his voice so only Melanie could hear. "Ever since she met that Scottish bastard, she's become bloody demanding."

Hiding her smile, Mel whispered, "I say good for her. And it could be worse; she could be mated to the Scottish leader."

Her dragonman made a low noise in his throat. "Don't tease me about that, little human. He's the last person I'd want as a brother-in-law."

She raised an eyebrow. "The last person? What about the leader of Skyhunter down south? I'm sure he'd be a fabulous relative to have."

Tristan narrowed his eyes. "It would still be a close contest between who would be worse."

Melanie laughed and then pushed against her mate's chest. He released his hold and she ordered, "Right, let's get something to eat before Arabella can escape. She loves her niece and nephew too much to leave with no one else to watch them."

As Arabella started to protest, Mel took Tristan's hand and ducked into the kitchen. Just as she's expected, having her mate close helped chase her worries away.

Releasing her hand to open the fridge, Mel watched as Tristan made her a sandwich. The everyday act soothed her fears a tad. Maybe she'd over analyzed things and everything would turn out all right in the end. Who would try to kill her over a book? Sure, a few authors had been targeted over the years, but Mel wasn't picking apart someone's religious beliefs. All her book did was talk about matings, celebrations, and clan structures.

Yet a small part of her knew someone would take offense. She only hoped it was an extreme minority. The dragon hunters already targeted them. Stonefire didn't need any more enemies to watch out for.

CHAPTER THREE

The next day, Tristan stood at the foot of the stairs waiting for his mate. Little had been said in the human media outlets about the release of her book. He wasn't sure if that was a good or bad thing, although it worried Mel to no end.

However, she had her first press conference in half an hour. That would be the first real test.

His human descended the stairs, wearing black trousers and a light green top that showed off her eyes. When she reached the bottom of the stairs, his gaze lingered on her chest before meeting her eyes. "That top is too tight. I don't want other males staring at your breasts."

Mel rolled her eyes. "This is probably one of the most conservative things I've worn in a long time."

His dragon huffed. *Her arse is highlighted too. I don't like it.*

His mate sighed. "I see your flashing dragon eyes. Tell him I'm wearing this and that's final. These clothes make me feel important, and I desperately need the confidence."

Tristan snorted. "Right, love, you lack confidence."

She poked him in the chest. "Sometimes, yes, I do. And since I'm about to represent our entire clan, I think you'd be a little more supportive."

"Agreeing with everything you say or do is boring. You wouldn't like it."

She sighed. "You're right, but matching wits with you is a wonderful stress reliever."

"So does that mean I have a free pass right now to tease you?"

"Most definitely not." The frown between her brows eased. "Are the twins still asleep?"

"Yes. Samira and Evie are in the living area, keeping an ear open."

"Where's Arabella?"

He shrugged. "She had things to do."

Tristan agreed with the look of confusion in his mate's eyes. Arabella spent most of her free moments with her niece and nephew. Maybe the humans gathering in front of Stonefire's main gate for the press conference had spooked her. He only hoped it hadn't reversed any of his sister's progress.

His mate took the last step down and patted Tristan's chest. "I bet Ara's afraid of how things could change. If humans and dragon-shifters eventually learn to interact freely with one another, she might feel the need to hide away again."

He growled. "I'm not about to let that happen."

"Me neither, but it explains her absence." Mel walked toward the living area. "I really wish she'd take up the foster position with Lochguard. A break from the clan might be good for her."

Tristan kept pace with his mate. "If she decides to go, then I'll allow it. But I'm not about to encourage it."

Mel glanced at him with raised brows. "Allow her? Tristan, love, remind me to tell Arabella about that the next time I see her."

"Aren't conversations between mates private?"

They reached the living area and Evie was grinning. "Maybe, but we heard it too. I'm going to make sure I'm here

29

when Melanie tells your sister what you said. I might even bring some popcorn."

His dragon growled. *There are too many females in this house. Let's hurry.*

I couldn't agree more.

Tristan touched Mel's upper arm. "Say goodbye to the twins and let's go. Bram's waiting for us."

Moving to the playpen used as a crib, Mel shot him a look. "I'm ready five minutes early, so hold your horses."

He fought a smile and lost the battle once Mel brushed the cheek of each of their babies in turn. He was a lucky dragonman, and he knew it, too. He only hoped the world would change for the better after the press conference instead of for the worse.

~ ~ ~

Standing behind the front gates of Clan Stonefire, Melanie struggled to keep her jaw from dropping. Bram had agreed to host a press conference just outside their land, but she had never expected the sight before her eyes.

There had to be at least a hundred people standing near the stage with the podium. Sure, the sunny July day was part of the reason, but the other had to be curiosity. She refused to believe it was to express their hatred or disdain, no matter how much Tristan seemed to think it would rear its ugly head sooner rather than later.

Bram stood to her left and Tristan to her right. Bram looked down at her. "Kai has his Protectors in position. So, are you ready, lass? Say the word, and we'll send them packing."

For a split second, Mel wanted nothing more than to hide away in her cottage with her mate and two children and forget all about the outside world. But what sort of life would that be? The thought of her children never embracing or getting to know their human halves helped chase away some of her nervousness. She was doing this partly for them, Murray, and all of the other dragon-shifter children in the world. They deserved a chance to live without daily fear of what could be done to their parents or even themselves when they reached maturity. Dragon-shifters should be admired for much more than the healing properties of their blood.

Not only that, but if things went well, she might finally have the chance to invite her family and friends to visit her. She loved her life on Stonefire and was grateful technology allowed her to communicate with her family, but sometimes she missed talking face-to-face with other humans about her old life.

None of that will happen unless you grow a spine and stand strong, Hall. Straightening her shoulders, Mel answered, "I'm ready. Let's get this over with."

Bram nodded. With Stonefire's leader on one side and her mate on the other, Mel felt safe. The two dragonmen would never allow anything to happen to her.

As they moved past the gate and toward the stage, the crowd fell quiet. The silence caused her stomach to churn and her palms to sweat.

Once Mel stood behind the podium, she forced down the butterflies in her stomach and took a deep, fortifying breath. Careful to project her voice since there wasn't a microphone, she addressed the crowd. "Thank you all for coming. My name is Melanie Hall-MacLeod and I'm the author of *Revealing the Dragons*. As much as I'd like to answer all of your questions, there simply isn't enough time in the day, especially as a mother of young twins." One or two women in the crowed smiled. That was better than nothing. She continued, "I'm going to give priority to those who have actually read the book. If you ask about my personal life, you lose the privilege of asking questions and I'll move on to the next person. Now, who's first?"

Twenty hands shot up as everyone asked questions at once. Picking one of the women who had smiled at her comment, Mel pointed. "Yes? What's your question?"

The rest of the crowd fell silent. At least, they were well trained. The woman with glasses and brown hair asked, "Your exposé makes the dragons appear almost human, except for a few minor differences. How do you respond to those who say your book is fiction and shouldn't be taken as truth?"

Mel was careful not to frown. "I have a degree in Social Anthropology. I'm trained to observe and record what I find, with the least amount of bias I can muster. While it's impossible to completely ignore my love for Clan Stonefire, I didn't write about my own family here. I wrote about the clan's history and practices as a whole. Those who wish to believe it's fiction will most likely never change their opinion, so it's pointless for me to worry about them."

The same woman asked a follow-up question. "I did talk to a former sacrifice, who recounted her time with Clan Skyhunter. Her account differs greatly, in that she was treated as a second-class citizen and pretty much shunned the entire year she was there. How do you respond to the other woman's statement?"

Evie had prepared Melanie for this question, so she answered without hesitation. "Each clan is semi-autonomous, almost like a country within a country. The easiest reference to compare are the Native American tribes in the United States. How one runs their tribe is different from another. Not all dragon-shifter clans will have the same opinions, customs, or behaviors. According to a former Department of Dragon Affairs official, Skyhunter has the worst track record for abusing the sacrifice system in the UK. A simple information request to the DDA would back up that claim, so I would take the former Skyhunter sacrifice's words with a grain of salt."

Nodding, the woman scribbled in her notepad.

From the corner of her eye, Mel saw a man push his way toward the front of the crowd and Tristan tensed at her side. She placed a hand on his arm in warning. The man wasn't a threat, yet. He might just want to move closer to have a better chance at having his questions answered.

She focused back on the crowd. Now that the first question was out of the way, her confidence was nearly back to normal. She could take whatever they threw her way.

Tapping the side of the podium with her right hand, Mel pushed on. "Next question?"

A bevy of hands shot up again. Melanie pointed to one of the men in the crowd. "You with the green tie, what's your question?"

Almost as if they had rehearsed, the crowd dropped their hands and fell silent again. The man with the green tie spoke up. "Is your book just a stepping stone into forcing Westminster to try to change some of the strict laws surrounding dragon-shifters?"

The same man from earlier inched closer to the front of the crowd. His short, dark hair made his blue eyes stand out, but nothing else about him was striking. His suit and tie combo were similar to all the other men in the crowd, yet his face was hard. The expression wasn't one she would expect to see on a journalist.

If his appearance wasn't strange enough, he had yet to raise his hand to ask a question.

Then the man's piercing blue eyes met hers for a split second and the hairs rose on the back of her neck. Even with the distance between them, she swore there was a burning hatred in his gaze.

A hatred she didn't understand considering she'd never met the man in her life.

Tristan squeezed her hand on his arm. Focusing back on the man with the green tie, she brushed aside the feeling for the time being. She needed to make a first good impression with the press. "I'm hoping to catch everyone's notice with my book. It's been thirteen months since I last hugged my mother and father because it's illegal for them to visit me. It's also been too risky for me to leave while I was pregnant and even more so now that I have young children who are half dragon-shifter. The journalists who came to Stonefire three months ago had special privilege; it's my hope that the same right is granted to those without political connections in the near future."

Mel scanned the crowd. Once she found the man with the dark hair and blue eyes, she kept her eyes trained on him. He was pressing even closer to the podium.

She said, "Next question," even though she knew who she would pick, if given the opportunity.

The man she'd been watching finally raised his hand so she pointed at him. "Yes, you with the maroon tie and gray suit."

Even though the man's expression was neutral, with no trace of the hatred from earlier, her intuition steeled her for the worst.

The man asked, "The humans and dragon-shifters have enjoyed the greatest peace in decades. Why risk the status quo?"

Some of the tension eased from Mel's body. His question was harmless enough. "Just because humans and dragon-shifters are killing each other less now than they have in decades doesn't mean it's peaceful. We should be working together for a better future, not hiding away in our own cultures, pretending the other doesn't exist unless it's convenient."

A male voice in the crowd shouted, "You should have become a politician."

Others in the crowd laughed. Mel smiled, but before she could reply, the man in the gray suit and maroon tie beat her to it. "Who wants a dragon's whore to represent them in Parliament?"

Tristan growled and she put a hand on his chest. Glancing over at her dragonman, she gave a small shake of her head. Then she looked back at the man in the crowd. "You're clearly one of those people who don't have an open mind and nothing I say will change it. I think you should leave."

From the corner of her eye, Bram signaled two of the Protectors standing guard around the crowd. The Protectors moved toward the man. They'd barely moved a few feet when the man raised a fist. In the blink of an eye, three people, in addition to the insult-throwing man, pulled out guns and fired. As the sound of guns being fired, mixed with screams from the crowd, Mel barely blinked before Tristan pushed her to the ground and covered her body with his. Her mate ordered, "Stay down."

Not wanting to be shot, Mel stayed put.

~~~

Tristan could smell blood.

It was too far away to be Melanie's but it still set off his dragon. His inner beast roared. *Kill the threats to our mate. Only because of me and my reflexes is she still alive.*

35

Rather than argue with his dragon, Tristan focused on what was important. *Killing them would put us in human jail. Do you want to leave Melanie and the twins on their own?*

Never.

Good, then let me assess the situation. I rely on your intuition and attention to detail. I will ask for your help soon.

His inner beast paced inside his mind. Leaving him be, Tristan rubbed his mate's arm with one of his hands as he whispered, "Are you hurt at all, love?"

Her voice wavered as she answered, "No, I'm fine. I had a feeling about that man, Tristan. I should've listened to my gut."

"The second he insulted you, a Protector should've gone after him. I'm going to have a word with Kai later."

Mel's fingers brushed against his forearm. "Between extra patrols on our borders in case of dragon hunter attacks and now this press conference, Kai is stretched thin. I'm not sure he could've done much more to prevent the shooting."

His dragon chimed in. *You should have allowed me to protect her.*

Don't start. Our mate needs us. Do you really want me to argue with you instead of taking care of her?

Silence was his answer.

Mel's fingers stroked his skin again. "Tristan? Is something wrong?"

"Sorry, love. My dragon isn't happy right now." Nuzzling her cheek, he added, "And I don't smell any death in the air. Bram and the Protectors should have everything in hand by now."

"Does that mean you'll let me up?"

"No, not until the shouting dies down. I won't risk you."

Under normal circumstances, his mate would argue. Her silence spoke volumes on how the shooting had unnerved her.

Content to protect his mate in silence, her scent calming his dragon down enough to avoid taking control, it wasn't long before Bram's voice filled his ears. "Tristan, Melanie, it's time to take you to safety."

Tristan turned his head to meet his clan leader's eyes but paused at the nick on his arm. The wound wasn't serious, so he wouldn't embarrass his clan leader by asking if he was okay. Instead, he demanded, "Are the threats contained? I won't allow Mel up until they are."

His mate huffed. "Tristan MacLeod, if Bram says it's okay, then let me up."

Bram nodded. "Aye, she's right. The threat is contained. At least, for now. I can't have my Protectors investigate the situation any further until you two are safe and out of the way."

His mate's voice was softer. "Tristan, please. I just want to go home and hug my babies, to reassure myself I'm still alive."

Unable to resist her gentle tone, Tristan pushed himself up and then offered a hand to Mel. She took it, and he hauled her against his side. His mate looked over to Bram and gasped. "Bram, you've been hurt. Are you okay?"

As his leader calmed Mel's fears, Tristan took the opportunity to survey the area.

The three human males and one female who had pulled out guns were currently pinned against a rock face about thirty feet away. Their hands were behind their backs. There was no way they were escaping in the near future.

His dragon snarled. *We should teach them a lesson so they will never again threaten our mate's life.*

The Protectors will do their jobs. We need to take Mel home.

His inner beast huffed. *Killing them is still the best option. What if they escape?*

37

That is highly unlikely. Now, shut it so I can take care of our mate. She needs us right now.

After his dragon grumbled his agreement, Tristan scanned the rest of the area to ensure there weren't any more threats. The human journalists were cordoned off to one side, with two Protectors talking with each in turn.

Despite the wide-eyed looks and fidgeting of the humans, any one of them could be carrying a weapon. All it would take was a good actor to fool the Protectors.

However, with the distance and two of the most senior Protectors watching them, Tristan was satisfied he could move Mel in safety. If any of them tried to pull a gun, Tristan would have time enough to shift. A stray bullet didn't stand a chance against a dragon's hide.

Tristan hugged his mate close and looked back to his leader just as Bram was ordering, "Don't tell Evie about the scratch or she'll find a way out here, Mel."

Melanie sighed. "Fine. But she'll find out sooner or later."

Bram gave a wry smile. "Aye, and I'll have hell to pay. I can handle it." Bram looked to Tristan. "We really should go now. I can escort you to the gate, but not all the way to your cottage. I'm needed here."

Tristan nodded. "Right, then let's go."

As they made their way to the front gates, Tristan's dragon spoke up. *I have memorized the faces of the threats. We can hunt them later.*

No. I'm a teacher, not a soldier.

I don't care. If another threat appears, I will fight you and take control.

38

REVEALING THE DRAGONS

From his inner beast's tone, Tristan knew his dragon wasn't making idle threats. *There will be no more threats. I will take our family to safety.*

His dragon grunted. *She will never agree to that.*

That doesn't mean I won't try.

Tristan tightened his grip on Mel's shoulder. When she looked up at him in question, he shook his head. He would fight the battle with his mate in private.

CHAPTER FOUR

Mel leaned against her mate the entire way home. His body was nearly as tense as hers, not that she could blame him.

Tristan would care nothing for his own safety. The tension was for her.

While a part of her loved him for his protectiveness, the rest of her wanted to sigh. A big fight was coming. Both man and beast didn't like threats to her life. Knowing her mate as she did, he would want to lock her away until everything was safe again.

Melanie didn't have that kind of time. There was a small window between the attack at the press conference and the various media outlets putting their own spin on both her book and the shooters. She needed to find a way to sway stronger support to her side.

An idea popped into her head, but she pushed it aside. She may want to change the world, but she wasn't about to exploit any of her friends to do it.

Try as she might, Mel still hadn't thought of a different idea by the time they reached the door to their house. At the sight of the two-story stone cottage, the attack and ideas of change faded and all Mel could think of was seeing her babies.

Rushing through the door past Evie and Samira, she raced into the living room and picked up her son. As she hugged the light, warm bundle to her chest and breathed in his baby-powder scent, Evie moved next to her. "Bram sent me a text, something about a shooting at the press conference. I pressed him for details, but haven't received a reply. What the hell happened?"

Since Tristan would embellish the danger, Mel recounted what happened minus Bram's wound, just like she'd promised.

Frowning, Evie crossed her arms over her chest. "I knew something like this would happen. I tried to persuade Bram to reach out and obtain permission to hold the press conference on Stonefire."

Opening her mouth, Tristan beat Mel to it. "That would've been even more dangerous. What if one of the shooters had slipped away? He or she could've gone after the young."

Evie was just as fierce with her reply. "I'm not daft, Tristan. They would've been subject to searches and pat downs."

Sensing a powder keg about to explode, Mel moved between them. "Stop it, you two. Not only will your shouting wake the babies, it's pointless. The press conference is over and done with. Now, we need to think of the future."

Tristan's gaze swung to meet hers. *Shit.* His pupils were slits. "Right, such as moving to Skye until Stonefire is safe again."

Only because of the baby in her arms did Mel keep her voice low. "No." He opened his mouth but she beat him to it. "I'm the one who put the clan in possible danger. I'm staying. I'm also doing my one-on-one interviews."

Tristan took a step toward her, his pupils at least round again. "Doing more interviews is mental and just inviting someone else to attack you. Unlike today, they'll be within arm's length. You won't have time to dodge a bullet then. Would you really risk making your children motherless?"

Narrowing her eyes, she somehow managed to keep from shouting. "Don't try and lay it on thick, Tristan MacLeod. I'm doing this for our children. You grew up on Stonefire's land and

41

are used to rarely venturing off it. But our children are half human, and they deserve the chance to get to know both sides of their heritage. I will fight to give them that chance, whether you like it or not."

Tristan took another step closer. "I want them to know their human sides as well, but not at the cost of your life."

She softened a fraction. "I'm not about to die, Tristan. I'm clever and have common sense. Let me try it my way, and if something comes up again, we'll revisit this discussion." He stood taller and she pushed on. "I didn't say I'd leave, but I'll at least consider sending Jack and Annabel away."

Tristan stared at her and her heart beat double-time. He was a protective male dragon-shifter; she knew that, but if she had to give him a time out to cool down, she would do it.

However, before her mate could respond, Evie cut in, her tone disbelieving. "Something else has happened."

Both Mel and her mate turned their gazes on Evie. Melanie asked, "What?"

Evie looked up, her face pale. "There was a BBC News alert. Both the London and Manchester DDA offices have been attacked."

Mel's remaining anger eased at the look on her friend's face. Evie loved living with her mate, Bram, but she had spent eight years of her life with the DDA before joining Clan Stonefire. "Is everyone okay?"

Samira touched Evie's shoulder and guided her to the couch. In the soothing tone she was famous for, Samira attempted to calm her. "Sit down, Evie, and tell us all about it."

Evie plopped on the couch and looked at Mel, Tristan, and Samira in turn. "Someone bombed the London office. In Manchester, there was a gun attack."

Mel moved to sit next to her friend. "Oh, Evie. I'm so sorry."

Strong, sassy Evie blinked back tears. The action squeezed Mel's heart.

Evie's voice cracked. "They don't know the extent of the damage or the number of casualties."

Mel placed a hand on her friend's cheek. "Do they know who did it?"

Evie shook her head. "Not yet. But given what happened here today, I have a feeling it's connected." Evie's eyes flashed with determination. "Neither the gun attack on humans nor the bomb are common M.O.'s of the dragon hunters. It must be one of the other anti-dragon factions."

While her friend didn't say it, Mel understood. "Probably brought on because of my book."

Evie placed her hand over Mel's and squeezed. "Don't blame yourself. If all it took was a book to bring about the attacks, then it was bound to happen eventually anyway. Crazies look for the smallest excuse to do their damage. Besides, if the DDA had planned to act indifferently about your book, that has now changed. You're about to receive more support than you ever dreamed of having for *Revealing the Dragons*."

Mel should feel elated, but the thought of it taking the deaths of innocent people to help her cause didn't sit well.

Jack squirmed in her arms before crying. Tristan, Samira, and Evie all moved to take him, but Melanie moved her son to her shoulder and stood. "I'll take care of him." She looked to Tristan. "See if Bram has a moment. He probably wants to know about the DDA attacks and Evie could use his support."

Evie opened her mouth in protest, but Tristan cut her off. "I'll find him."

As her mate turned and left, their daughter woke up too and cried in unison with her brother. With a sigh, Mel pushed on to take care of her children. Events were snowballing fast. She soon may not have the opportunity to take care of, let alone cuddle, her children over the coming days. She would treasure what time she had remaining.

~~~

Tristan picked up his pace toward the main gate. Each step away from his family went against his instincts, but Bram needed to know the information about the DDA office attacks.

While he grudgingly accepted Evie as Bram's mate, he wasn't close with the human female. Only because Melanie had asked him had he gone. Otherwise, the bloody woman would do it herself.

His dragon pushed to the forefront of his mind. *You were unable to change her mind. If danger shows up, I will make sure she goes to safety.*

No.

She will die because of your carelessness.

Untrue. Your ways will chase her away. She won't stay if she feels contained. Do you want her to leave us?

She is our mate. She won't.

Rather than argue, he threw the beast into the back of his mind. At least, the attacks had been in Manchester and London. He didn't enjoy other people's deaths, but the distance eased some of his fears about his mate's life. No doubt, the attack on the press conference earlier was connected to the other two attacks, which meant Melanie wasn't the sole target.

Revealing the Dragons

Tristan reached the gate and was waved through by one of the Protectors. Scanning the grounds, he saw Bram talking with Kai, Stonefire's head Protector. He moved in their direction.

Once he approached, Bram looked up and frowned. "Tristan, why are you here? I know you want to help with those who threatened your mate, but the best place for you to do that is at her side."

Tristan grunted. "Your mate needs you."

Bram turned to face him, his eyes searching Tristan's. "What happened? Is she okay? Is it the baby?"

"Evie is physically fine. And far as I know, she still carries your young."

"Then start talking because that was unnecessary," Bram spat out.

"This wasn't the only attack today. There was a shooting at the Manchester DDA office and a bomb went off in London. Your female is upset."

Kai jumped in. "Do you have any details?"

Tristan shook his head. "No, it was some kind of vague news alert."

Kai looked to Bram and said, "Go to your mate. I can take over here and I'll also see what my contacts from my army days can tell me."

Bram nodded. Once Kai took out his mobile phone and walked away, Tristan looked back to his clan leader. "Have you found out any more information about the attack here?"

Bram motioned his head toward the gate. "Let's walk and talk." As they moved, Bram continued, "The four shooters are currently with Zain. They haven't been forthright, but if anyone can get them talking, it's that towering dragonman."

Zain was one of the Protectors who had proven his interrogation skills four months ago, when Bram's mate had been kidnapped. "Your mate doesn't think the shooters are dragon hunters."

His clan leader glanced at him. "I agree, but my mate does have a name, Tristan. Would it kill you to call her Evie?"

He grunted. "She is your female and your mate. I will never harm her, but the only human female who matters to me is Melanie."

Bram gave him a wry look. "Don't let Mel hear you say that."

Tristan ignored his friend's comment. "If it's not the dragon hunters, then who do you think the shooters work for?"

"It could be any of the extremists, ranging from the old Order of the Dragon Knights to the ultra-conservative Purist Party."

"Politicians don't plan attacks like the one today. Also, the shooting was very amateurish, which rules out any group with a deadly reputation."

Bram raised an eyebrow. "I agree about the gangs and groups with reputations, but don't dismiss the politicians so easily. They may not have planned the attack themselves, but if they can nudge any of their supporters to do so, the politicians can then use the events to their advantage."

"I have no interest in human politics, so I can't comment on that. But if we rule them out and the organized crime groups, could something similar to the Order of the Dragon Knights still be around? While no one will put on steel armor and go on quests to slay dragons, a group hiring out to destroy the dragons' way of life is a possibility."

Bram shook his head. "I haven't heard of anything. Maybe if we ask Evie's friend, the one with far too much knowledge about our kind; she could tell us something."

"Isn't the human female in hiding?"

"Yes, but from the brief exchanges I've had with Evie's friend, Alice, hiding won't stop her from finding out what she wants to know. If a rumor is floating around, she'll know it."

Tristan frowned. "Even so, I don't like rumors. Is there any proof?"

Bram shook his head. "No, but we'll wait to see what Kai and the news has to tell us. I'm sure Evie can contact Alice in a few hours and see what the human has dug up by then."

The conversation lulled and they continued in silence. Since Tristan and Bram had been friends for nearly thirty years, it wasn't strained. Still, since his friend was also mated to a strong human female, Bram might have some advice on how to handle Melanie if Tristan managed to ask.

Before he could think better of it, Tristan blurted out, "Would you force your female into safety, even if she didn't want it?"

Bram stopped and Tristan followed suit. His leader searched his eyes a second before saying, "If I could actually see the threat coming at her, then yes, I would. However, if the threat is merely there without any specifics, then no. Evie is like Melanie and would hate me if I stashed her away against her will. Melanie loves you, Tristan, but being a prisoner would slowly eat her alive. She needs to interact with people, especially with you. While you may not like it and your dragon screams to take her away, work with her or else you could lose her."

She will not leave us.

Shut it, dragon. You're no bloody help.

With a growl, his beast retreated again.

Bram continued to stare at him, waiting for a reply, so he murmured, "I will take that into consideration."

Tristan walked and Bram caught up in two strides. His friend added, "I already contacted Finlay Stewart about the attack. Relations are friendlier between the Scots and Clan Lochguard, something about fighting against the English centuries ago created a tenuous bond that still exists, and he's confident enough to send some assistance. While he can't come here himself to help this time, he'll send the same Protectors who came before to help with security. Barring any attack from the air, Mel and your children should be safe."

Tristan believed his words and that confidence eased his tension slightly. "Thanks, Bram. I just can't lose her."

Bram clapped him on the shoulder. "I know, Tristan, I know. I feel the same way about Evie."

Tristan's dragon huffed. *Take our mate to Skye. We won't lose her then.*

There's more than one way to lose a mate, dragon.

They reached Tristan's home. The instant they were inside the door, Bram called out, "Evie Marie?"

Carrying Murray on her hip, Evie walked over and laid her head against Bram's chest. As the clan leader soothed his mate with words and touch, Tristan went into the living area.

Melanie sat on the couch with Annabel asleep in her arms. A quick look told him Samira had Jack in the armchair off to the side.

Taking his son from Samira, she stood and smiled. "Now you're back, I should go home. Liam's waiting for me." Samira looked to Mel. "Will you be fine without me?"

Mel smiled. "Of course. Go to your family. Tristan can handle the other half of baby duty for now."

Once Samira was gone, Tristan moved to sit beside his mate, wrapped his free arm around her shoulders, and she laid her head against him. She sighed. "Thank you for bringing Bram here."

"I know better. Five more seconds, and you would've handed me the crying baby and gone out the door to fetch Bram yourself." He squeezed her shoulders. "Did you find out anything else about the attacks while I was out?"

"No. Evie couldn't contact her friend currently in hiding; you know the one with all the knowledge about dragon-shifters? She's worried something's happened to Alice."

Tristan rubbed his mate's arm. "The female has remained hidden for nearly a decade. I'm sure she's fine."

Melanie leaned into his touch. "I sure hope so."

Bram appeared in the doorway with his son in one arm and hugging his mate with the other, his face grim. "Kai just sent me a text about the attacks."

Tristan raised an eyebrow. "And?"

Bram let out a sigh. "The Order of the Dragon Knights are claiming responsibility for the attack."

CHAPTER FIVE

Careful to keep her voice low so as to not wake the babies, Melanie asked, "The same Dragon Knights as the ones in the legends old William tells when he drinks a little too much?"

Bram nodded. "And while most humans believe them to be legends, the Dragon Knights were real. They disappeared three hundred years ago thanks to pressure from Enlightenment thinkers and scientists who wanted to save the dragon-shifters from extinction. Because of their centuries of silence, I'm taking their claims of responsibility with a grain of salt."

Mel blinked. "Wait a second. In all of my research, no one ever mentioned the Knights being real. Why not?"

Tristan squeezed her shoulder and she looked to him. "Because, love, we believed them long gone and didn't want to give anyone ideas about starting something similar again."

Melanie eyed her mate. "You're not supposed to keep secrets from me, Tristan."

Uncertainty flashed in Tristan's eyes, but Bram spoke up before her mate could answer. "It was on my order, Mel. A clan leader's word is the only thing that outranks a mate's."

Her throat closed up at being excluded, but Mel pushed it aside. "So you still don't think of me as one of the clan? Or that I could know a secret and keep it? As you've seen today, this book's release has caused major damage and threatened my life. Complete honesty is the least you owe me."

Bram shuffled his feet. Evie elbowed him and after a quick glance to Evie, Bram focused back on Melanie with regret in his eyes. "I'm sorry, lass. The decision was made shortly after you conceived, when you asked about writing the book. Between the increase of dragon hunter attacks on our borders and Evie's kidnapping, I forgot all about it. I'll rescind the order with the entire clan as soon as the threat passes and it won't happen again."

Bram's words eased some of her hurt. "I need some answers now, Bram, or I can't help and think of a way to tackle the threats."

Stonefire's leader nodded. "Ask away, then, lass. I have a few minutes."

Facts were more important than dwelling on the past slight, so Mel continued, "Right, then, let me get this straight. Not only do we have the dragon hunters wanting to trap all of you and drain your blood, we now have knights who want to slay you? For what purpose? Killing a dragon won't bring them prestige."

Bram answered, "I'm sorry, lass, but you're wrong about that. In addition to earning a reputation in criminal circles, because killing a dragon is bloody difficult to do, they'll gain prestige with their fellow knights. If they truly are back, they'll be competing against each other and then it won't be long before they have fans romanticizing them and admiring their work from afar."

Evie spoke up. "Why the bloody hell would someone cheer on slaying dragons? If nothing else, their healing blood would be wasted."

Bram drawled, "Nice to see you equating us with other medical rarities and not as individuals."

Evie slapped her mate's chest. "Stop it, Bram. From a logical perspective, slaying a dragon makes little sense anymore. They can't win trophies or the respect of a king or nobleman. Not to mention it's illegal and will bring the DDA down on them."

Mel remembered something from her time working with Evie over the last few months. Leaning forward slightly, she looked to her friend. "But didn't you mention the next-in-line at the DDA wanted to dismantle the sacrifice system and pretty much destroy the DDA? Jonathan something or other."

Evie's mouth dropped open for a second before she regained her wits. "Jonathan Christie. He'd have knowledge of the old Dragon Knights. Not only that, but by attacking the London DDA office, he's sure to have killed the head of the DDA, Regina Ward."

Mel frowned. "Does this Christie bloke have connections to pull something like today off?"

Evie shrugged. "I have no bloody idea. The man was far up the hierarchy. I only saw him from a distance at department-wide events."

Tristan jumped in. "This is nothing but conjecture. Where's the proof?"

Bram shook his head. "We just came up with the theory, Tristan. Gives us a little time to prove it."

Mel pushed past her mate's words. "If we can prove it and Christie is behind the Dragon Knights' return, then we have a bigger problem." She looked back to Evie. "If the head of the DDA is dead, then who is in charge?"

Evie's face turned grim. "Jonathan Christie."

Mel continued. "Right, so if he's in charge, he'll ignore the Dragon Knights and they'll continue making terrorist attacks. No human female in her right mind would volunteer to be a sacrifice.

Revealing the Dragons

Rather than becoming targets, the sacrifices and their families would turn to the black market for dragon's blood."

Bram nodded. "Right, which benefits the hunters."

Stonefire's leader looked to his mate. "At one point, you mentioned the possibility of Simon Bourne working with the authorities to look the other way for his dragon hunts. Maybe it went all the way to the top levels of the DDA. That could explain the laxness of arresting dragon hunters over the last few years."

Evie placed a hand on Bram's arm. "Maybe, and it's bugged you for months why my rescue was so easy. Do you think it was a distraction, to give Simon Bourne or Jonathan Christie a chance to recreate the Order of the Dragon Knights? They might've had this attack planned for months to coincide with Mel's book launch and needed to ensure no one made any sort of connection between Christie and Simon Bourne until they could pull off the attacks."

Bram frowned. "Maybe. Although I don't like making assumptions without proof. I need to talk to Kai." He looked at Evie. "And we need to contact your friend. The more information we have, the better we can face this possible new threat."

~~~

Despite the possible conspiracy brewing amongst the ranks of the DDA, all Tristan could think about was his mate.

He didn't like the way Mel was slowly moving away from him. It might only be an inch or two at a time, but he knew it was because he'd hurt her.

His dragon paced. *You should have listened to me. She might leave us because of your actions.*

53

She won't. And listening to you meant disobeying Bram. Dragon-shifters need a clan structure to survive or it will become chaotic.

A real dragon wouldn't hide anything from his mate. It is the way it's supposed to be.

Right, so his dragon was now giving him the guilt trip. *I will handle this. Be quiet so I can listen to the conversation.*

With a huff, his inner beast moved to the back of his mind just as Bram mentioned needing to talk with Kai. Then Bram looked to Melanie and added, "Keep a watch on the human media for me and if you could come up with any ideas on how to use it to our advantage, let me know. I'll be back as soon as I have more information."

Mel gave a stiff bob of her head. Tristan wanted to rub her back to help ease her tension, but as she scooted another inch away from him, he decided against it.

Bram looked to him. "Tell Melanie whatever she wants to know. There won't be any more clan secrets kept from your mate. She is one of us."

Once Tristan nodded, Bram turned toward the door. "Keep your phones close to hand. Evie or I will call you soon."

As Bram left with his mate and son, a strained silence filled the cottage. He wanted to ease his mate's pain, but Tristan had never been very good with words. He had no idea of what to say, yet if he said nothing, he might lose her trust.

Unsure of what else he could say, Tristan blurted out, "I'm sorry."

Mel turned toward him, her eyes guarded. "Right here, right now, I need to know if there's anything else you've been keeping secret from me."

"Just one more thing."

She moved another inch away. "Well?"

He glanced down at his son, asleep in his arms. The sight of his son's peaceful face gave him the courage to look back at Melanie and say, "After Annabel was born and I waited to see if you'd live or die, I cried to the point of nearly sobbing. I hadn't done that since my mother's death."

Mel's posture eased. "Tristan."

She would probably allow him to hug her and hold her, but he needed to do more than patch up his mistake; he needed to heal it. "I'm sorry I didn't tell you about the Dragon Knights, Melanie. Bram's dominance and my respect for his leadership prevented me from giving in to the desire to share everything with you. I won't do it again. Please don't leave me or take away our babies."

His mate frowned. "What the hell are you talking about?"

"You're angry and keep moving away from me. I keep waiting for you to bolt."

"Tristan MacLeod, stop being paranoid. I'm upset, yes, but I would sure as hell hope our love is stronger than one little incident. Things have been nearly perfect up until now. Something was bound to happen. However, if you're willing to give up on us that easily, maybe I should leave."

Tristan reached out and touched her cheek. "No, I don't want you to leave. You and the children are my everything."

Her face softened. "There's that tenderness again. It wouldn't hurt to show it a bit more often, you know, when I'm not angry?"

"So, you forgive me?"

With a sigh, she moved, readjusted her grip on their daughter, and cuddled her head against his chest. "I suppose so, but to start making it up to me, tell me everything you know about the knights."

He kissed the top of his mate's hair. The heat and softness of her against his side allayed both the man and beast's worries. "There's not a lot to tell, really. The modern human sacrifice system was loosely based on one used during the medieval period, when lords and villages would offer a human female in exchange for protection against outside threats. The Dragon Knights thought they could do a better job of protecting other humans, at a price of course.

"The legends say the knights slayed the dragons to prove how much better it would be to hire them for protection than to offer a female to a dragon-shifter for the same thing."

His mate nuzzled his chest with her cheek. "Bram mentioned the Enlightenment-period thinkers saving the dragon-shifters. Is that when your number repopulated, even without human sacrifices?"

"Yes. At least, until the two world wars during the last century. After that, we were desperate again."

"I know the rest from my research, about the local bargains being made on a case-by-case basis until the DDA was established in the 1980s. If only I had access to some of the university libraries, I could start digging for references. Just think, Tristan, there's a whole side to human and dragon-shifter history which the humans know nothing about."

She fell silent and the corner of his mouth ticked up. "Are you outlining another book in your head?"

Looking up, she gave a coy smile "Maybe."

He chuckled and kissed her nose. "Let's handle the aftermath of this one first, love. Then we'll tackle the next."

His mate snuggled against him again. "I love you, Tristan. And I wish we could just stay like this, cuddled all day with our children, but Bram asked for us to watch the human media reports. We should get started."

Tristan growled. "If you want up, then give me a kiss first."

"How about asking nicely?"

"No." He moved his son on his lap to lean against his sister in Melanie's arms and then placed his finger under Mel's chin. "This time, I'm going to take what I want."

Tilting her head up, he kissed her. She allowed his tongue in without protest and he made each stroke count, letting his mate know how much he loved her better than he could ever do with words.

~~~

When Tristan finally broke their kiss, Melanie sighed. "One day, you're not going to make me forget everything with a kiss, Tristan. What will you do then?"

His eyes flashed to slits and back. "That day will never come. My dragon agrees with me on that."

With a smile and a shake of her head, Melanie readjusted her children so they were both on Tristan's lap. "So cocky." As Tristan placed a hand behind the heads of each of their twins, her heart squeezed. "Yet so devoted."

Before her mate could persuade her to do some more kissing, Mel moved to the TV and turned it on. The BBC was in the middle of a special news report. Settling back beside her mate, Melanie tried to make sense of the images dancing across the screen.

Judging by the fire brigade trying to put out the flames of an old, brick building, the scene was the London Department of Dragon Affairs.

Pushing aside her initial shock, Melanie focused on what the announcer was saying.

"We're still waiting on an official count, but sources say the death toll might reach as high as two hundred people. The Chief Fire Officer has put out a public statement asking citizens to please stay away from the scene. Memorials and tributes will be scheduled at a later time, once the fires are out and the investigation is complete."

The announcer went on to replay the Chief Fire Officer's earlier statement and Mel looked up at Tristan. "Two hundred people dead in London alone."

"I know, love. But they're talking about you now. Look."

Mel glanced to the TV. Her official author photo was in the corner. She focused on the announcer's words.

"The group claiming responsibility, the Order of the Dragon Knights, put out a video stating the recent book about the dragon-shifters living in the North of England is what prompted the attacks. Quote, 'The dragon-shifter book is part of their agenda to seize control of the country. Melanie Hall-MacLeod was probably forced to write the book of lies under duress, to help alleviate the truth of dragon brutality. As soon as we let down our guard, the dragons will attack.

"The Department of Dragon Affairs has long worked with the dragons and can't be trusted. To ensure the safety and future of the United Kingdom, we will target anyone helping the dragon-shifters, be it a civilian or the government. Consider this your only warning. If you associate with dragons and no longer wish to become a target, then comment on this video posted online with details of traitors. We will be checking there as well as other major sites on the internet, to be announced at a later date.'"

The announcer introduced a guest analyst and Mel clenched a fist. "How dare they accuse us of trying to take over the country, let alone plan an attack." She looked up at Tristan. "Do you see now why I have to do the interviews? Otherwise, the knights will receive all of the airtime. The most easily swayed section of the population will start to believe them before long."

Tristan sighed. "Even if you do the interviews, it's going to take more than you defending yourself and the book to change public opinion. The knights have emotionally charged material."

Her idea from earlier popped into her head. Could she really exploit her friends to sway public opinion?

"Melanie." She met her mate's brown eyes and he continued, "Tell me what you're thinking so I can help you. Something's conflicting you. It's plain on your face. What is it?"

"Sometimes, I wish I was better at hiding my feelings."

"Stop stalling. Tell me what's on your mind, my little human."

After a deep inhalation and exhalation, Mel blurted out, "I have an idea, but it involves Nikki, baby Murray, Charlie's mate, and..."

He raised an eyebrow. "Who?"

"Arabella."

Her mate raised his other eyebrow and she spilled her plan. When she was finished, he sighed. "It might work, but even if Bram gives the okay, you'll have to convince Ara to help you. And honestly, I'm not sure if she will."

"I know, but I have to try, Tristan. I don't know what else to do."

"Right, the twins will wake up soon to be fed. Once that's done, we'll ask Ella and her mate to watch the babies and then we'll talk to Bram."

She gently touched her daughter's head. "Do you think Bram will agree?"

"I don't know, but even if he does, Ara will take some work."

"Then I'll just have to try my best. If we don't garner more support, then the dragon-shifters might be worse off than ever before."

Tristan kissed the top of her head. "Even if it does, we're survivors. Now, take Annabel and I'll take Jack."

Mel picked up Annabel, who didn't so much as bat an eyelash. The second Tristan moved Jack, however, the boy started wailing. He didn't like missing his sleep.

As they moved and took care of their children, a sense of guilt about what she was about to ask her friends made her stomach churn. If there were any other way to sway public opinion, she would do it.

There wasn't, so she hoped Arabella MacLeod was strong enough to possibly get them out of the current mess. The Dragon Knights needed to be dealt with swiftly. She refused to think about what would happen if her sister-in-law said no.

CHAPTER SIX

Two hours later, Melanie sat in Bram's cottage with Tristan at her side. One of the teachers who worked with Tristan agreed to watch the twins for a few hours, allowing Mel and Tristan to pitch their idea to Bram.

It hadn't taken long to convince Stonefire's leader of the merit of her idea and they'd been interviewing the necessary players ever since.

Mel looked over at the black-haired, brown-eyed young Protector talking with Evie near the door. The young dragonwoman, Nikki, gave Melanie one more look with a nod of acknowledgment before she left.

Shutting the door, Evie walked back into the room and sat on the arm of Bram's chair. She snaked her hand around the back of Bram's neck before saying, "Nikki's agreement makes three out of four. Do you think you two can convince Arabella?"

Mel glanced to Tristan and her mate answered, "Not only is Bram allowing Murray to be a part of this, Bram supports the plan as well. That may be the tipping point in garnering her consent."

Mel squeezed Tristan's hand in hers. "We'll find out soon enough. She's due any moment." Melanie looked to Bram. "You still haven't told me why you're going with my idea. A few seconds after I finished, you began calling the others to come in. Why?"

Stonefire's leader shrugged. "You made a good case. A leader's best asset is realizing when to lean on his clan members for help. I'm not about to be a macho alpha who needs to think of everything myself. Somehow, I don't think Evie would put up with it."

Evie leaned slightly against him. "I'm glad you understood that on your own."

While Mel and Evie hadn't hit it off in the beginning, Mel couldn't think of anyone better suited for Bram. She only hoped Arabella would find the same happiness one day.

Guilt made her stomach churn. Mel had spent more than a year coaxing and pulling Arabella out of her shell, yet what she was about to ask might undo all of that hard work. Still, even if her sister-in-law grew to hate her afterward, Mel would suffer the ill feelings if it meant earning the public's support and ensuring the safety of Clan Stonefire.

A knock at the door interrupted her thoughts. Evie went to answer it.

Tristan squeezed her hand and whispered, "You can do this, love."

After giving her mate a weak smile, Arabella's voice carried down the hallway. "Anyone care to tell me why I had to trudge all the way here? I'm on a deadline for upgrading our security systems. With the new threats, I can't afford to let it wait."

Evie guided Arabella inside the living area. "Believe me, Arabella, this is more important."

Arabella looked at each of them in turn before replying, "Okay, the look on Melanie's face alone has me worried. What's wrong?"

Tristan rubbed her knuckles with his thumb. The rough, warm strokes gave her the courage to spit it out, "You've heard of the attacks today, but have you heard about the Dragon Knights claiming responsibility?"

Arabella glanced to Bram and he nodded. "She knows all about them now."

Arabella looked back to Melanie. "Of course I know. Everybody knows, but what does that have to do with me?"

Mel sat up a little taller. "Everything. You're part of the solution."

Arabella frowned, her scar crinkling slightly in the process. "What the bloody hell are you talking about?" The dragonwoman looked around the room. "Someone tell me what the fuck is going on and quickly because I have shit to do."

Tristan growled, "Watch your language, Arabella Kathleen MacLeod."

Arabella rolled her eyes. "The world is falling apart and you're worried about my language." The dragonwoman's brown eyes moved to Mel's. "Tell me straight, Melanie, as you always do. I don't like this beating-around-the-bush bullshit."

With a deep breath, Mel knew her sister-in-law was right. "I need you to go on live TV and tell the world about what was done to you when you were attacked by the dragon hunters."

Arabella blinked. "What?"

Mel's voice was soft when she replied, "I know it's a lot to ask, but there's a plan behind it, Ara. Will you listen?"

Arabella shook her head and took three steps back. "Absolutely not. What happened to me is private." Arabella looked to her brother. "Why would your mate even suggest it, Tristan? You, of all people, know how difficult it's been to overcome that trauma. I don't understand why you would ask this of me."

~~~

Tristan was careful to keep his face neutral despite the protectiveness screaming for him to take care of his younger sister. "Every second of airtime the knights receive, the more people will start to believe them. The only way to counter their tactic is to give the public something to care about. The brutality of the hunters will earn us some desperately needed sympathy."

Ara narrowed her eyes. "Sympathy? Do you really think I care about what the humans think? They not only did this to me, they killed our mother, Tristan. I'm not about to be used as a freak show for your plans."

Melanie leaned forward, but Tristan gave his mate's leg a squeeze to stop her. He continued, "You're not a freak show, Ara, but a survivor. If there was any other way, we wouldn't be asking you to do this. But the BBC interviews are in two hours and we need an answer."

Before Arabella could reply, Bram jumped in. "Listen, Arabella MacLeod, your clan needs you. Hell, your family needs you. If you thought what happened to you was bad, what if that happened to your niece and nephew? Or, how about to your brother? Even me? Would you want that?"

Even Tristan sat up taller and tapped his hand against his thigh at the dominance in Bram's voice. Unsurprisingly, Arabella bowed to her clan leader too as she mumbled, "No."

Bram raised an eyebrow. "Right, then you're going to help us, along with Nikki, Charlie's mate, and even wee Murray. It's not just about you, Arabella, it's about allowing the world to see what's happened and hope like hell they will believe us. More importantly, that they'll support us and turn against both the hunters and the knights. I want the same future as Melanie, where humans and dragon-shifters get along better than they do now.

Only when humans may come or go as they please on our lands will we not have to rely on a barter system to ensure the survival of our race."

As Bram and Arabella stared at each other, Tristan's dragon peeked out. *Arabella's dragon is scared.*

How in the hell can you know that?

I just do. Be careful with her.

I'm not about to coddle her. I did that for a decade and it hurt her in the long run.

Just remember to support her. She will need it.

Before he could decode his dragon's cryptic words, Ara stood a little taller and raised her chin. "If I do this, then I want a guarantee I can be the first to foster with Clan Lochguard."

Tristan blinked. "What? Where did this come from?"

His sister pierced him with a stare. "Finn invited me several months ago and I've been thinking about it ever since. I want to go."

Narrowing his eyes, Tristan growled, "What did the Scottish bastard say to you? I sure as hell hope you don't fancy him, Arabella. He's not right for you."

Anger flashed in Arabella's eyes. "How do you know what I bloody want? I'm not the same dragonwoman I was a year ago, Tristan. I need a change. Besides, I've always wanted to go to Scotland. Your mate's memories with her family only made me want to go more."

He opened his mouth but Melanie laid a hand on his leg. Looking over at her, her brows furrowed. "Don't glare at me, Tristan MacLeod. Scotland is a beautiful place and I would say the same to anyone." He mumbled an apology and Mel continued, "Arabella's made her decision. Let her go to Lochguard." His mate glanced over at Bram. "Provided, of course, Bram says it's okay."

Bram shrugged. "Arabella is a grown dragonwoman. I may have mixed feelings about the Scot, but he would never allow harm to come to the lass. Of that, I'm sure. As long as there's not immediate threat of violence, she can leave in two months' time. I'll tell Finn myself after the interview."

Melanie looked over to Arabella. "Then we have a deal, Ara."

Feelings Tristan couldn't decode flashed across his sister's face. He swore happiness was one of them. *Fuck.* He didn't care for that. Yes, he wanted his sister to be happy, but not with another clan. Arabella was his only link to both their parents and the past. If she moved away for good, a part of him would go with her.

His sister straightened a little more. "What do I need to do?"

Mel answered, her voice gentle. "Think of the simplest way to describe what happened to you and your mother. I want to break down the myths of dragon-shifters being beasts without any feelings. Your pain is real, Arabella, and it may convince people to reevaluate what they know about dragon-shifters, maybe even view you as more human."

Ara crossed her arms over her chest. "Even with me supposedly pouring my heart out, it's going to take more than that to change decades, hell, centuries, of fearing us."

Melanie leaned against Tristan's side. "We thought of that already. Do you have time to upload a three-chapter free sample before the interview? I want to offer a site to download it during the interview. Nothing fancy, just a way to read the most powerful chapters from my book. I think they may change more than a few minds."

Ara sighed. "Fine, I'll do it. Just make sure you keep my brother off my back. I don't want him trying to change my mind about Lochguard in the coming weeks."

Tristan frowned. "You're my sister. I just want what's best for you."

"I'm nearly thirty years old, Tristan. I can handle myself."

He opened his mouth, but Mel squeezed his arm and shook her head. He shut his jaw. If his sister wanted to get her heart broken by the flirting bastard, then by all means, he'd let her. Then she might listen to him next time.

Bram broke the silence. "Right, then we have a plan. Since there are less than two hours to put everything in place, let's meet back here in an hour and a half for a pre-interview meeting. I hope like hell this will work."

Melanie melted against Tristan and murmured, "So do I, Bram, so do I."

~~~

Melanie stood in front of her closet trying to decide which clothes would complement exploiting her sister-in-law's past when Tristan wrapped his arms around her from behind. His breath was hot against her ear as he whispered, "You're tense, love. Let me help you relax before the interview."

His hand snaked to her breast and squeezed. Melanie ignored her nipple going hard and swatted his hand. "There's too much to do in the next hour. I don't have time for a quickie."

Her mate nuzzled her neck and she leaned against his broad, muscled chest. She never tired of the contrast of her curves against his muscles.

His voice rumbled against her back. "Are you sure? You're thinking too hard and if you go on like that, you'll only be at one hundred percent instead of one hundred and twenty percent."

Taking a few extra seconds to soak in the feeling of being surrounded and fondled by her mate, Mel mustered the strength to push at his hand. Tristan released her and she turned around to cup his face. "I appreciate it, I do, but sex will have to wait, love. I need to coach some of the others right before the interview, which means getting my shit together now."

Her mate grunted. "I think after you finish sorting the business related to this book, you need a break, my little human."

She glanced at him. "Maybe a week or two, but I'll go crazy if I don't have something to do just for me. You'd feel the same way if you couldn't teach anymore."

Moving to the dresser a few feet to her side, Tristan leaned against it. "Maybe. But promise me we'll have some time together with just you and me. Then maybe I can help alleviate some of your stress."

Turning toward him, her voice was dry. "What, with your cock?"

When Tristan grinned, she had her answer. "Men. The world's going to pot and you're thinking of sex."

"Hey, you said yourself you missed not having to squeeze it in between naps or feedings. I'm just looking out for you, love."

"Yes, but of course." She rolled her eyes. "Once everything is fine and dandy again, we'll look into it." Mel turned back toward her closet, plucked out a dark purple blouse, and said over her shoulder, "Did you check in on the news like I asked?"

"Yes. There are some protests breaking out near the DDA offices in London and Manchester, although it's still quiet in

Edinburgh, Cardiff, and Belfast. The tide is turning faster than I like in England."

"Well, from the history I've been able to dig up, the English hold a deeper fear of the dragon-shifters than the other countries of the UK. They are easier to rile up."

"It could also be because England has the biggest population of the four countries, which means more idiots to believe everything they see on the telly."

Mel shrugged. "Maybe, but I think it's more to do with the power of the dragon hunters in England as well as Skyhunter's treatment of female sacrifices." She turned to look at Tristan. "Convincing Clan Skyhunter to play nice is something else we need to add to the list of things to address."

Tristan shook his head. "Good luck with that, love. Marcus rules that clan with fear."

"Well, we'll worry about that later." Shucking her top and throwing on the purple blouse, she did up the buttons. "Hopefully, the BBC interviews will at least put Stonefire in a better light." She finished the last button and looked up. "I need you to believe in my plan, Tristan. You do believe in me, right?"

Tristan walked over and traced a finger down her cheek. "Of course, Melanie Hall-MacLeod, I will always believe in you."

Her heart warmed at his support. "Thank you." She gave him a quick kiss before adding, "Are you ready? We should go."

"The interview isn't for an hour."

"I bet Bram is ready early and I could do some practicing with him and Evie."

Her mate raised an eyebrow. "Not with me?"

"No, you're still being super nice to me because of what happened earlier and I need some straight up honesty."

"I can be honest."

She smiled. "I know, but not for this. Besides, I need you to check on Arabella before she reaches Bram's cottage. She may have a backbone now, but we both know she still has nightmares and fits occasionally. As much as I need her help, I don't want to send her into a catatonic state. I'm sure Finlay Stewart wouldn't like that."

Tristan grunted and Mel bit her lip. "You're going to taunt me with your ridiculous theories concerning him and my sister, aren't you?"

"But of course. I live to tease you."

Tristan placed his hands on her hips and pulled her against him. Leaning down, his breath danced across her lips. "Just wait, love. When your brother is older, then maybe I'll set him up with a dragonwoman and tease you. We'll see how you like it then."

"Oliver is nearly seventeen. By the time he's old enough for your plan, Arabella will be mated to the Scot and have lots of babies. You'll be calling Finn your brother."

"Don't even joke about it. He's not right for her."

"Says the man who hated humans and look who you ended up with. Sometimes, a person doesn't realize what they need until it happens."

Tristan made a low noise in his throat. "Aren't you wise and savvy today?"

She ran her hands down his chest. "But of course." Giving him a pat, she pushed away. "Go wait for Samira and Ella to show up to watch the babies and then go to Arabella's place. I need to finish getting ready."

After a slow, lingering kiss, Tristan whispered, "You'll be brilliant today, love, so stop worrying."

"And there you are, still trying to make up for earlier."

He growled. "Remind me not to compliment you any more today, then."

She grinned. "Maybe later."

He gave her one more quick kiss and then disappeared out the door. Alone in the bedroom, Mel faced the mirror. "Right, Hall, stop worrying. You'll be brilliant."

With a nod, Melanie finished getting ready for possibly the most important hour of her life.

Chapter Seven

Arabella MacLeod arranged her long, black hair around her face and neck to cover her burns and part of her scar. Except for the small, thin line of the scar running across her nose and upper temple, she almost looked normal. She could piss off her sister-in-law and keep her hair covering her old wounds for the upcoming interview. It would be a form of payback for asking her to do the bloody thing in the first place.

Yet if she did, Bram and Melanie could rescind their promise to allow her to foster with Lochguard.

She very much wanted to go, too, and not for the reasons her brother assumed. While Finlay Stewart was the first strange male who hadn't caused a panic when touching her, Arabella wanted something much more. She wanted freedom.

Even the discussion an hour or so earlier had knocked against the freedoms she had while she remained on Stonefire's lands. As long as she lived in the Lake District she would never be free to make her own choices without someone hovering over her.

Finn's words from a few months ago popped into her head. *"I don't know about you, but living day in and day out with everyone walking on eggshells must be exhausting. Yes, you've gone through something terrible. But isn't it time for you to face the world and live your life?"*

Revealing the Dragons

Pushing her hair back from her neck and face, Arabella stood up tall and straightened her shoulders. As much as she hated to admit it, the Scottish leader was right. If it took a few minutes of humiliation to earn freedom for at least six months, she would take it. Once she was on Lochguard's land, she could make a go at starting over.

Since she lived a mile from Bram's cottage, she headed out early to ensure she would arrive on time.

Outside, the jagged peaks and flat, green stretches looked just as they had for her entire life. Yet if she fostered with Lochguard, she wouldn't be able to see the comforting sights anymore. Surely, since Lochguard was situated deep in the Highlands, she'd have new sights to memorize.

Before she could recall any of the pictures she'd researched online, two dragons flew overhead. Watching the green and black beasts alternate between beating their wings and gliding, a longing Arabella hadn't felt in over a decade bubbled up. She wanted to fly again.

Her usually silent dragon said, *We can do it anytime you're ready.*

Ara stopped in her tracks. She could do as she normally did and ignore her inner beast, or she could reply.

The thought of talking to her dragon brought back memories of the last time they'd had an actual conversation. She'd been screaming in pain and her dragon had tried to calm her.

Closing her eyes, Ara clenched her fist and willed the memories away. Her racing heart told her that if she didn't act quickly, she would slip into a panic attack.

Bram would never allow her to foster at Lochguard if he saw her lose control. Breathing in and out, she focused on the rustling of the wind through the trees and the warm July breeze against her skin. After a minute or two, her memories faded.

Anxious, her dragon hovered on the edges of her mind. The beast wanted to comfort, but was afraid her words would make Arabella's attack worse.

Arabella teetered on the edge of talking with her dragon when her brother's voice boomed, "Arabella, why are you standing with your eyes closed?"

Her eyes snapped open. Sure enough, Tristan was walking toward her with his brows drawn together. Frowning, she barked, "Trying to forget I have a brother."

He stopped in front of her, studying her intensely. "I think you're lying, but somehow, I don't think you're going to tell me the truth."

"It's none of your business. Why are you here, anyway?"

"Mel wanted me to check on you."

Normally, she'd just ignore the comment and change the subject. For some reason, she couldn't do that and blurted, "And you wonder why I want to go to Lochguard. I'm not a child, Tristan."

He raised an eyebrow. "Are you able to talk to your dragon yet?"

"I—" She didn't want to lie to her brother. "Almost."

"Right, then how about when you can talk to your dragon like a proper dragon-shifter, I'll loosen the reins."

"Or, I could just wait it out. Once I'm in Scotland, I won't have to put up with your judgmental bullshit."

Her brother growled. "Watch it, Arabella. Going to Scotland isn't set in stone."

Rather than have a pointless argument with her brother, Arabella walked ahead. Her brother took a few strides to catch up before he said, "Forget Scotland for now. Are you going to be able to do this?"

She glanced over. "It's not like I have a choice. Bram and Mel pretty much decided it."

Her brother's eyes softened. "If there were anyone else, Ara, I would ask them. But this is the best chance at a decent future for my children. They, and all dragon-shifter children, need you to be strong."

She blinked. "Tristan MacLeod is giving talks of encouragement? Who are you and what did you do with my growly, verbally stunted brother?"

When he growled, she laughed. Tristan smiled. "It's nice to hear you laugh again, Arabella."

Being sentimental with her brother wasn't Ara's specialty, so she changed the subject. "I'm ready, Tristan. Let's get this over with."

He nodded and as they walked in companionable silence, her tension eased and her worries faded. She even dared to hum inside her head for her dragon. Her inner beast hummed back and Arabella smiled. She would be honest during the interview and let the humans know about some of the horrors practiced on dragon-shifters. It was time for the human world to stop pretending the dragon hunters weren't real.

After that, she would soon have her freedom.

~~~

Mel watched from the window as a group of dragons took turns flying passes over the front gate. She was no stranger to the sight of flying dragons, but the ones in the air above her had on a new kind of armor over their chests, bellies, and lower necks. Bram said the synthetic shields protected against air projectiles. Considering she'd seen the laser gun damage up close when

Tristan had nearly died a year ago, she hoped the new armor was effective.

Moving from the window, she went to the monitor displaying the front gate security feed. Bram had wanted to keep an eye on things, in case they turned south. Already, a crowd of about twenty people stood in front of Stonefire's land.

Sure, no one in the crowd was throwing grenades or launching firebombs, but it could happen any second. Or, maybe they were waiting to view the interviews and then react. Thanks to the convenience of technology, everyone would check out the live broadcast using their cell phones.

A van drove up the single road leading to Stonefire's main entrance. When it was close enough, the crowd cleared a pathway. She couldn't see the side of the van, but it would be the BBC since no other interviews were scheduled for the day.

Mel turned away from the monitor and paced. She'd prepped everyone except Arabella, who still hadn't arrived. There was nothing for her to do but wait and it was driving her crazy.

As she shook her hands and wrists to loosen up, there was a knock on the door. Bram entered with Murray in his arms. Blue eyes stared at her as he sucked his thumb. Mel smiled. "At least Murray seems in a good mood."

Bram shrugged. "He usually is. Nikki and Hudson are waiting downstairs with Evie. She's doing her best to calm them, but maybe you can help. They're nervous as hell."

"Any sign of Tristan and Arabella?"

"No, but don't worry, lass. Ara will come."

"I hope so." She glanced to the monitor. The van was no longer there, which meant it had to be on Stonefire's lands. "The interview crew will probably be here any second."

76

"Melanie." She looked at Bram, his gaze steady and strong, every ounce the clan leader he was. "Whatever happens today, I want to say thank you for everything you've tried to do for our clan."

"Things could go very wrong, Bram. I wouldn't be thanking me just yet."

He took a step toward her. "Even if planes appear in the sky and start dropping bombs, I'm still going to say thank you. You are giving it a try, which is more than anyone else has ever tried to do for my kind."

She tapped her hand against her thigh. Accepting praise had never been one of her strong points. "It's a bit selfish, you know, since I'm mostly doing it for my children."

A corner of Bram's mouth ticked up. "Tell yourself that, lass, if it helps." He paused and then continued, "Are you coming? Everyone's moving toward the temporary green room, which will probably make Nikki and Hudson even more nervous. I'm sure Evie's pregnancy hormones aren't helping the situation either."

She laughed. "At least, she's not pregnant with twins. I'm told it makes everything twice as bad, although I'm not sure I believe Tristan." She stood up tall. "At any rate, let's get this party started."

Bram chuckled. "Act just like that, and everyone will love you."

"Maybe. I'm going to have to be somewhat diplomatic when talking with the journalist."

As they walked out the door and down the stairs, Bram said, "I've watched Jane Hartley's interviews before. She's more than fair."

She glanced over at her clan leader. "I'm not worried much about her. I'm more worried about the aftermath."

Bram kept his voice low. "Just keep that feeling to yourself, lass, or the others might start panicking."

She nodded right before she and Bram entered the room being used as a waiting area; all three sets of eyes fixed on her with expectation. Nikki and Hudson's eyes also held a hint of nervousness. They wanted her to allay their fear.

For the first time, she understood what Bram must deal with on a regular basis.

Gathering up every ounce of no-nonsense she possessed, Mel gestured toward Nikki and Hudson. "The TV crew should be here soon. But no worries, I know you all will be brilliant. We've gone over your talking points. If you freeze, take a deep breath, and try again. All of Stonefire is depending on us."

Looking a little pale, Nikki and Hudson both nodded.

While Mel had seen Nikki fairly often after being assigned as Evie's guard, Mel had rarely talked with Hudson in the past. His mate, Charlie, had been a Protector and died while in the hands of the dragon hunters four months ago. His poor mate had been drained of blood.

The dragonman was quiet, with sadness in his eyes and permanent smile lines at the corners of his mouth. At one time, he must have been happy. However, she had a feeling he hadn't smiled in months. She hoped he remedied that soon for the sake of his son.

Nikki, on the other hand, was naturally outgoing and quietly bubbled with a mixture of excitement and nervousness in her eyes. Even though she had been captured at the same time as Charlie, Nikki had survived. However, not even Melanie knew all of the details from her time with the dragon hunters.

Before Mel could think of more encouraging words to give the nervous dragon-shifters, Kai walked into the room and everyone looked to the head Protector. "We've searched and patted down the BBC crew. There weren't any weapons, nor was there any scent of drugs or chemicals. That's as much as we can do."

Bram nodded. "Right, then show them into the living area. That's where the interviews will be held. Tell them we'll be there in a few minutes."

Kai left to carry out his order

Melanie resisted the urge to fidget. Pulling Bram aside, she whispered, "Where's Arabella?"

He handed Murray over to Evie. "I'll ring Tristan while you keep everyone calm. Can you manage that?"

"Yes."

"Good, then I'll be right back."

Once Bram left, Mel shared a glance with Evie. Even her friend was a little worried.

No. Mel wouldn't give up. If Arabella truly wanted to foster with Lochguard, she would pull through. She had to.

~~~

Tristan wanted to rush around the last corner and guide Arabella into the house. The interview should have already started and he wanted to watch his mate.

His sister, on the other hand, was in no hurry. Just as they reached the last bend, Arabella stopped and clenched her hands. Careful to keep his impatience from his voice, he asked, "Is something wrong?"

One beat of silence went by and then another. Finally, his sister said, "I don't know if I can do this, Tristan."

The earlier confidence and fire was gone from her voice. Turning toward his sister, he saw her looking at the ground. The sight reminded him of Ara in her late teens, during the first years after the attack.

His dragon chimed in. *She needs us, like in the old days.*

I know, bloody dragon. Give me a chance to help her.

Then stop dawdling.

To quiet his dragon, Tristan walked over to his sister. Placing a finger under her chin, he raised her head until she met his eyes. The uncertainty and sadness lurking in her brown gaze squeezed his heart. "Arabella, you can do this. And not just because of the deal you made with Mel and Bram. You've come a long way in the last year. Talking about your past will bring you into the final stretch of your recovery."

"I'm afraid of another attack hitting me when I'm on camera. The memories are hard to handle one at a time. How can I handle them all at once?"

He placed his other hand on his sister's shoulder. "Think of Lochguard. Hell, think of the flirty Scottish bastard if it'll help. Visualize something you want, something positive, to counter the bad memories. Then you'll do fine."

Ara searched his eyes before replying, "This is your teacher persona, isn't it?"

He shrugged. "Some of my students are afraid of their inner dragons until we work together to make them friends. Or if not friends, then to the point where they tolerate one another. I gave you too many years of space, but not anymore. Before you go to Lochguard, we're going to work on you and your dragon."

He waited to see if he'd pushed too far. The present might not be the best time to suggest working together with her dragon, but Tristan didn't care. Pushing Arabella would let her know he wasn't going to coddle her again.

His sister's eyes turned determined. "I was too embarrassed to ask for your help before. Now that you've offered it, I'm going to take it."

"You're the only blood family I have, Arabella. Never be afraid to ask me for something."

The corner of her mouth ticked up. "Even if it's the middle of your date night with Melanie?"

"There are some conditions. However, if your life depends on it, then yes, I'd leave to help you."

They each stared at one another. If Melanie were here, she'd be gushing about love and family bonds. Tristan and Arabella didn't work like that.

Instead, he squeezed his sister's shoulder and motioned toward the direction of their destination. "Are you ready then?"

After a deep breath, Ara nodded. "I think so."

"Good. Then it's time to make the dragon hunters wish they never messed with our family."

They began walking again and his sister looked up at him. "That's a bit much, Tristan. One story won't change the world."

"I don't know about that. If Melanie's involved, it just might. The bloody woman wants to change all of British society in less than two years."

Arabella smiled. "That sounds like she has another book waiting to be written."

He shook his head. "Don't even bring it up. I'm going to try to distract her once all of this is over."

They reached the door of the cottage and Kai waved them inside. The head Protector guided them to a room off to the side as he briefed them. "Melanie's in the other room and is about to go on air. Arabella will be last." A guard moved from in front of the door. As they entered, Kai continued, "Wait in here with the others. They can tell you more of what to expect."

Tristan looked to Kai. "Are there any signs of danger?"
The blond dragonman shook his head. "So far, so good.
Security is on high alert. Nothing will happen to your mate,
Tristan, if I have anything to do about it."

Kai looked as steady and serious as always, but Tristan
noticed the circles under his eyes. The head Protector was
working around the clock and probably not sleeping.

He would mention it to Bram later. An overworked
Protector was a liability rather than an asset, and Kai was too
valuable an asset to burn out.

Tristan replied, "I believe you. Go do what you need to do.
I'll keep Arabella company here."

The undertone was that Tristan would make sure his sister
stayed put.

Once Kai was gone, he looked around the room until he
saw Nikki, Hudson, and Evie holding baby Murray, all standing
near a TV monitor. Evie looked over her shoulder, smiled warmly
at Arabella, and then met his gaze. "Mel's interview is about to
start. Come watch."

Guiding his sister to the group, he looked to the telly and
saw Mel. She looked a little too attractive with her hair done and a
light coating of make-up, but he contained his dragon before his
beast could complain. Instead, Tristan held his breath as the
reporter started talking.

CHAPTER EIGHT

To keep from fidgeting, Melanie wiggled her toes inside her shoes. When wiggling wasn't enough, she tried to tap each one in turn. The wait was killing her, and not just because Arabella hadn't arrived by the time she'd been taken from the ad-hoc green room.

No, she would both help the dragon-shifters and change history for the better, or she would fuck up and make them worse off.

If anyone had ever told her she would be at this critical juncture in dragon-shifter history, she would've laughed them off a few years ago. Funny how trying to save her brother had brought her to this exact point in her life.

Soon, the female journalist she'd been briefed about, walked into the room and Mel focused on doing the best job possible.

The black-haired, blue-eyed woman smiled and extended her hand. Once Mel took it, the journalist said, "My name is Jane Hartley. Thank you for agreeing to talk with me."

"I should say the same for you. I really appreciate you coming at such short notice."

Jane waved a hand in dismissal. "You're giving me a leg up on everyone else. I should be the one thanking you." She motioned toward the groups of chairs. "The live broadcast will start in a few minutes. Let's get settled."

Mel took one of the seats and crossed her legs at her ankles. Glancing at the two cameras, she tried not to panic. She'd taken on human-hating Tristan and won. Surely, talking about one of her passions in front of a live broadcast would be easier.

At Jane's voice, Melanie looked at the woman. "If possible, look at me and not the camera. We go live in thirty seconds."

Nodding, Mel counted down in her head. When the cameraman did the final finger countdown and then pointed at them, she sat a little taller and looked at Jane as directed.

Jane looked just past Mel's shoulder into one of the cameras. Each second they sat in silence only made her heart beat faster. How long did they have to wait before they could get the interview started?

After about forty-five seconds, the woman finally replied to whomever was talking to her via the earpiece. "Thanks, John. Melanie Hall-MacLeod first came here as a sacrifice and mated the dragon-shifter assigned to her a little less than a year ago. She is the author of *Revealing the Dragons* and she, along with a number of other Stonefire clan members, have agreed to talk with me and give us a glimpse into the lives of a few dragon-shifters." Jane looked at Melanie and smiled. "Before we begin, is there anything you would like to add?"

A million thoughts raced through her head. She wanted to dive right into a speech, but decided against it. The journalist might be smiling for the moment, but who knew what could happen five minutes in.

Mel took a deep breath through her nose to settle her stomach and replied, "No, so far, so good."

"Right, then my first question is why did you write the book? There are a number of theories and rumors floating around, as you well know, but what is the truth?"

Mel kept her voice strong. "The truth is I wanted to share how the dragon-shifters live here so everyone can see they're not so different from us. There is no ulterior motive, no plan for world domination. Anyone who says otherwise is just being silly."

"You must admit that a person who can change into a fifteen-foot dragon in a matter of seconds is scary to regular humans. If the government were to allow dragon-shifters and humans to interact freely, how would we prevent rogue dragons from terrorizing the population?"

Anger coursing through her body, Mel squeezed her leg with one of her hands to help tamp it down. Her voice was calm yet steely when she replied, "Human psychopaths roam the street and more than a few are killers. Yet do you put away all humans with a temper to prevent a future possible murder? No. It's the same with dragon-shifters. There are a few bad eggs, but as you'll see with some of my clan members today, dragonmen and women are just trying to live their lives without being hunted, targeted, or drained of blood."

"I assume you're talking about the dragon hunters and the problem of them selling dragon's blood on the black market. Rather than us talking about it from secondhand knowledge, how about we bring out one of your clan members?

Her part of the interview seemed extremely short, but there wasn't anything she could do but nod. Maybe she'd have a chance later to talk more about her time with Stonefire.

From the doorway on the far side, one of the BBC staff guided in Hudson. Once he sat down next to Melanie, Jane smiled at the dragonman and started up again. "Hudson, thank you for meeting with us. I understand dragon hunters killed your wife a few months ago. Please, tell us what happened."

Mel watched Hudson recount the story as they had rehearsed. The dragonman was solemn and his voice only cracked twice during his retelling. Melanie's heart squeezed at the pain in his eyes. She didn't know what she would do if she lost Tristan.

Still, since she'd heard the story ten times before, her mind wandered once Jane asked him a few more questions. Had Arabella arrived yet? Would she even go through with it?

No. Stop doubting yourself. Tristan will take care of it. If anyone could convince her sister-in-law to do something, it was Tristan. And even if he had trouble, he'd call Bram.

Focusing back on Jane and Hudson, Melanie pushed thoughts of Arabella out of her head. Whatever her sister-in-law ended up doing, her clan members needed her support.

~~~

Arabella watched first Hudson, then Evie with Murray, and finally Nikki leave with one of the news staff. As each of her clan members left, it became harder not to bolt. It was nearly her turn.

Melanie had been fantastic in her section of the interview, being both strong and passionate without devolving into petty comments. Her sister-in-law might have been a politician in another life.

Her other clan members had done fairly well, too. Even when Hudson broke down when describing his mate's death, Jane Hartley had even reached out to comfort him, not caring he was a dragon-shifter. If that had been the response of a seasoned journalist, then the general human population had to be moved as well.

Mel's plan might be working, even without Arabella's help. She eyed the door. If she left now, she would still have time to leave the cottage before they called her.

Then Tristan walked into the room with Bram and any hope of escape faded. The only two males in the entire clan who could convince her to carry on with the interview had arrived.

Bram moved to her left and Tristan to her right. Bram was the first to speak. "You still up for this, lass?"

"Like I have a choice."

Bram studied her before replying, "You have a choice, Arabella. If you want to go to Lochguard, you'll do this. If you wish to back out, I'll support you, but that signals you're not ready to leave the clan."

She looked back to the TV screen. Nikki had become quite animated, gesticulating with her hands and moving her arms to describe how the dragon hunters had captured her.

Tristan's voice garnered her attention. "You'll do fine. Remember what I told you."

Right, positive thoughts. She recalled her research on Clan Lochugard.

The Scottish clan was situated in the northern Highlands, nestled next to a lake. Peaks and rolling hills surrounded the clan lands. While similar, the lake and hills were different from the Lake District and more than anything, she wanted the chance to explore them. With time, maybe even fly over them.

Then Finlay Stewart's handsome face flashed into her mind, and she only just prevented herself starting. *Why am I thinking of him? He's bossy, pushy, and far too cocky.*

Out of nowhere, her dragon said, *But he is fun to tease.*

She paused a second before forcing herself to reply. *W-what did you say?*

Don't fear me, Ara. We will have fun in Scotland.

Arabella blinked. A part of her wanted to keep talking with her dragon, but another part of her felt odd. While her inner beast had been there all along, they were essentially strangers and she had no idea how to act.

Yet she'd just talked with her dragon for the first time in almost eleven years. A deep-seated loneliness she'd ignored for so long eased a fraction and her heart warmed.

The feeling prompted her to stand a little taller. She'd come a bloody long way for her recovery. If she truly ever wanted to heal, she needed to leave Stonefire for a while and figure out who the hell she was, as well as what she wanted from life.

One of the news staff entered the room and motioned for Arabella to follow. She could feel both Tristan's and Bram's eyes on her, so she looked to each one in turn. "I'll be fine."

As she walked to the staff member, Arabella admitted she had no idea what would happen after the interview, but she did know one thing. She would finish the interview and go to Scotland in two months' time.

She was tired of fear and hiding. From here on out, she was determined to be whole again.

~~~

Tristan waited until Arabella was out of earshot before he looked to Bram. "She'll be fine."

"I sure hope so, Tristan. Dangling Lochguard like we did just doesn't seem right."

"It's the only thing she truly wants. Much like Mel forced her way into Arabella's life, she needs to be pushed in this, too. I'm sure you saw her eyes flashing to dragon slits."

"Yes, but I'm going to give her a few tests before she leaves. She won't know that's what they are, but I don't want her breaking down in front of Clan Lochguard. Her pride may never recover."

"We can discuss that later. Right now, I want to listen to my sister and mate, so shut it."

Bram shook his head, but remained quiet.

On the TV, Arabella sat down in the final chair, the furthest from both Melanie and the journalist. At least the distance kept the human from touching Arabella, which was one less possible trigger for his sister's past trauma.

Tristan crossed his arms over his chest and moved his gaze to his mate's face. Few would be able to tell, but she was gripping her leg tightly to restrain herself. Jane Hartley had barely talked to Melanie. His mate wouldn't like that one bit.

When Arabella started talking, he listened. "Yes, my name is Arabella MacLeod and I was taken, beaten, and tortured by a group of Carlisle dragon hunters when I was seventeen years old."

Even though Arabella's voice was a little less confident than he liked, Tristan was proud of his sister.

Jane asked, "Is that where your scar and burns came from?"

Arabella paused and then replied, "Yes. A group of men held me down, poured petrol on half of my body, and set me on fire."

The journalist paused. Her voice was soft when she finally spoke, "Did they give a reason?"

Tristan gripped his arms tighter. *As if they needed a bloody reason.* Dragon hunters were evil.

His sister, however, was more diplomatic than he was. "A dragon's blood can't heal anything until a dragon-shifter hits maturity. Melanie stated as much in her book." Arabella glanced to Melanie and then back to the journalist. "They wanted to weaken me so it would be easy to keep me captive until I hit maturity."

Jane Hartley cleared her throat and asked, "Some say we already spend too much money tracking down the dragon hunters. What would you say to those people?"

Arabella frowned. "After today, I would hope they'd think twice before saying such crap. Each of us here has suffered because the laws surrounding the dragon hunters are too lax. Human law prevents us from taking care of the threat ourselves, so the law either needs to be changed or the DDA offices need to step up their game. Too many dragons are dying because of the limbo we're placed in."

Bram murmured, "She's doing extremely well. If she'd never been attacked, she might've been like this always. She might even have gone after the clan leadership."

Tristan's dragon spoke up. *I agree with Bram. Arabella is more of a leader than anyone admits.*

She's kept herself locked up for years. Of course they would think so.

She will do extraordinary things in the future. I believe in her.

Before he could think too hard on his dragon's words, Jane was talking straight to the camera again, signaling the end of the interview. Tristan focused on her words, "I wish to thank all of our guests for sitting down and talking with me. I'm sure I'm not the only one who will do some thinking and reevaluate my views on dragon-shifters, dragon hunters, and their interactions with humans.

"If you're curious to read more, you can download a free three-chapter preview of Melanie Hall-MacLeod's book, *Revealing the Dragons*. The web address is on your screen, or you can go to our website for the link.

REVEALING THE DRAGONS

"Stay tuned for the hourly news update with John Smythe. This is Jane Hartley reporting from Clan Stonefire in the Lake District. Good evening."

The screen switched to another program and Tristan moved to the door. He needed to check on his mate and his sister. Judging by Melanie's face, she wasn't happy about the whole thing and he wanted to calm her down before her temper got the best of her.

CHAPTER NINE

Melanie forced herself to smile and shake hands with Jane. As soon as she could extricate herself, Mel moved toward the far door.

She still couldn't believe the bloody woman. Mel had barely said a few sentences the whole time. How was she supposed to make a passionate speech and sway hearts and minds if all she did was sit there?

Not paying attention to where she was going, she rammed into a hard chest. She was about to apologize when she saw it was her mate. "Tristan."

Without a word, he engulfed her in his arms and hugged her close. The contact helped to ease her angry tension a fraction. Her mate's voice rumbled in his chest. "You were brilliant, just as I thought you'd be."

She looked up, glanced around, and whispered, "I barely did anything. She wouldn't let me talk. The speech I rehearsed was all for nothing."

One corner of Tristan's mouth ticked up and she glared. Ignoring her glare, he said, "You did fine. The stories from the others were more powerful than anything else."

She let out a deep breath. "I know, but I wish I could've done more. Still, Arabella was fantastic. She didn't break down once. She's come a long way from the first day I met her, Tristan. She's ready to go to Lochguard."

Her mate grunted. "We'll talk about that later. For now, I want to get you home. There's bound to be a response to what was said during the interview and we should be ready."

Mel looked behind her, but Bram was talking with Evie and Arabella. Nikki and Hudson were already gone. "We should invite your sister."

"I think she's already going with Bram and Evie. Knowing my sister, she wants to make sure Bram puts in a call to Lochguard without delay."

Sure enough, Arabella waved a hand at them, turned around, and left.

Tristan moved so that he was at her side with his arm around her shoulder. She sighed. "Do you think the dragon hunters, or even the newly reformed Dragon Knights, will retaliate now?"

As they maneuvered to the front door, Tristan squeezed her shoulder. "I don't know, love. But if I know Kai, he's already planning defensive and offensive strategies."

"Is that why he was standing off to the side for awhile, inside the interview room, staring at the journalist? So he could gather information for his plans?"

"What are you talking about?"

Mel leaned a little more against her mate. "Well, he stood with his arms crossed and stared at Jane Hartley the entire time. Has the clan worked with her before?"

"Not to my knowledge. He was probably just keeping an eye on you. As much as we'd like to trust the BBC, not everyone will have pro-dragon views."

"If you say so. Still…"

"Spit it out, Melanie."

"Well, it was hard to see because of the bright lights shining on me, but I swear he was looking at Jane like he was starving."

They were out in the open air now and Tristan stopped them to look down at her. "What?"

She tilted her head. "Yes, he looked like he'd been waiting his entire life for her and given the chance, he would've devoured her."

Tristan shook his head. "Impossible. He met his mate a long time ago, but he couldn't have her for some reason."

"Do you know why not?"

He raised an eyebrow. "Have you met Kai? At times, he makes me look chatty."

She smiled. "True." She wrapped an arm around his back and gave a small push. Once they were walking again, she added, "I'll still ask Bram about it, later. Provided, of course, we're not under attack."

At the mention of danger, they walked in silence.

Melanie picked up her pace. As curious as she was about Kai, she was even more curious about the reaction to their interview. She just wanted to cuddle her children, sit next to her mate, and find out what their future held.

~~~

An hour and a half later, Mel was waiting for the relief gel to start working on her son. When they had come home, Ella had suggested the boy was teething. Checking his gums, which were warm and slightly swollen, Mel knew it was true.

Leave it to Tristan's son to make a fuss when he didn't feel well. Father and son were identical, in that regard. Annabel also had warm gums, but her daughter was taking it a hundred times better than her brother.

Rocking her baby boy, hoping the soothing gel would help Jack fall asleep, she looked over at Tristan. Her mate was grinning at her. He cuddled Annabel tighter to emphasize he had the sleeping half of their children.

Mel scowled and Tristan grinned even wider. "Don't look at me like that. You're the one who volunteered to take Jack. He'll fall asleep eventually."

"Gee, thanks. While I do this, I don't know, maybe you could check the news and see what's happening? An hour and a half is enough time to delay the inevitable."

"If it weren't for the children and the impending doom for all dragon-shifter kind, I'd rile you up more. I like it when your eyes flash and your face flushes."

She sighed. "Please tell me you aren't thinking of sex right now, Tristan."

He shrugged. "Hey, when a dragonman has a mate as beautiful as you, he always thinks about sex."

Battling a smile, she lost. "Just turn on the TV and check the news."

Tristan chuckled. She knew he'd be cocky and bloody unbearable when they were alone later in the evening.

Picking up the remote, he waved it toward her. "I wouldn't worry too much. Bram and Kai would've come banging on our doors if something were wrong."

"Still, I want to know. If things aren't going as well as I like, I have to think of something else."

Tristan raised an eyebrow. "We all will think of something else. Taking on the world by yourself will kill you, love."

Jack squirmed in her arms as if he were going to wake up so she bounced him. Once he settled, she looked at Tristan. "If it means you'll turn on the damn TV, then I'll agree to a costume party meeting."

He gave her a once-over. "That I would like to see."

Mel rolled her eyes and she heard the TV blip on.

Looking to the TV screen, the view was Stonefire's front gates. The sight of the crowd made her stomach drop. Were they waiting to attack? Or, were they just curious?

Then she looked at the crowd more closely. Some people were holding signs, but she couldn't quite make them out. Since the crowd members were waving and moving around, it was difficult.

Finally, after stepping closer to the TV, she could read one, "Stop the Torture." Another one read, "Justice for Arabella."

Mel blinked. "Am I going crazy or does Arabella now have a fan club of sorts?"

Tristan grunted. "It seems so. I'm not sure how I feel about that."

A voiceover started and she waved a hand at Tristan. "Shush a second. I want to hear what they're saying."

For once, her dragonman didn't challenge her.

The voiceover filled the silence. "No one was certain of how our earlier interview with members of Clan Stonefire would be received. Yet a scant two hours after the broadcast, a group has already assembled outside Stonefire's gates. The crowd, while still small, is passionate about justice for the dragon-shifters. Our own Jane Hartley is at the scene. Let's go to her now to hear what some of the participants have to say."

The screen changed to show Jane Hartley's smiling face. "I'm outside Stonefire's gates, and as you can see, there is a crowd of about fifty people behind me. Unlike the incident with the press conference, all of the people behind me appear to be supporters of the dragon-shifters. A few of them have agreed to talk with me. Let's talk to our first person now." Jane looked over and the shot panned out to include a woman wearing glasses. Jane asked, "Why did you decide to drive out here today?"

The woman's voice was from the North, probably from a neighboring village. "Hearing those stories on TV made me feel ill. When one human kills another or sets a woman on fire, they are brought to justice. Yet we never hear of dragon hunters or haters being brought to justice. It's time to change some of the old laws, especially given what happened to the DDA offices earlier today. Something needs to be done."

Jane asked, "Have you been a life-long supporter of dragon-shifter rights?"

The woman wearing glasses shook her head. "I never thought much about it, to be honest, until I moved nearby and could see the dragons fly overhead. Even then, it was just something to gawk at. After hearing the four stories today, however, I can't ignore them anymore. I want to know them better."

Closing her dropped jaw, Mel looked to Tristan. "Did you hear that? I almost want to say it's too good to be true, but maybe, just maybe, things will finally change."

"I wouldn't get your hopes up just yet. It's still early."

"Even so, the fact so many came out to support us is a sign. Some of the indifference toward dragon-shifters is fading. That alone is huge."

"It would be even better if they left my sister out of this."

Mel let out a sound of frustration. "Can't we just celebrate a little? Yes, I know things could go wrong at any minute, but I can't remember a time in my life when people cared this much about dragon-shifters."

Tristan looked at her a second before replying, "I will hold off for a few hours, at any rate. If things continue as they are, and that's a big if, I might even have a chance to intimidate your parents and brother in person before long."

Mel rolled her eyes. "My mom is a lot like me. She won't put up with your crap."

"Your brother then."

Mel smiled at the mention of her brother. "I'm not sure about Oliver. He used to be funny and able to charm anyone before the cancer. I wonder if he's back to his old self or not. It's hard to tell during our video chats."

"If you have anything to say about it, we'll find out soon enough in person, my little human."

Smiling, she looked down at Jack, who had finally settled. "Let's put the twins down and risk searching the internet. I want to know how other news outlets are handling all of this, and not just in Britain. Maybe then you'll be a little more optimistic."

"You need my doubts to ground you."

Schooling her face into a mock serious expression, she made her tone sarcastic. "Yes, without you, the world would never change. Only through your doubts can I be motivated to change the world."

"Bloody stubborn woman." Tristan stood up carefully. "Going back to your original topic, America might handle it well. I'm not so sure about China or Russia, though."

Dropping her mock act, Mel walked with her mate up the stairs to the twins' room. "Regardless, if we figure out which countries are taking it well, Bram can reach out to some other clan leaders."

Tristan's voice was dry. "Does Bram know of your plans for world domination?"

She shot a look over her shoulder. "Not yet. But he's the one who wants to form alliances. This is too good of an opportunity to pass up. I'm pretty sure Evie will back me up on this. If she does, he doesn't stand a chance."

Shaking his head, Tristan mumbled, "Human females."

"That's right, mister, and you wouldn't have it any other way."

Inside the room, Tristan gave her a quick kiss. "As much trouble as you are, you're right. Both man and dragon only want Melanie Hall-MacLeod."

"You're not too bad yourself, dragonman."

Laughing, the pair of them went to work putting the twins down for the night.

Mel kept touching each of her babies in turn. All of Tristan's teasing aside, their children would have the future they deserved. If, for some reason, the public's response became tepid and unsupportive, Mel would think of another tactic. And then another. She would do anything to ensure her children would have the opportunity to know their human side of the family.

She and Tristan might even be able to start their own yearly family summer trips. Even though her twins and mate could fly, nothing bonded a family like a long car trip.

With both babies asleep in their cribs, she leaned over them and put every ounce of confidence she had into her voice as she whispered, "I will change the world for you two, no matter what it takes."

~~~

Arabella uncrossed her arms and widened her stance. Then she shuffled her feet and clenched her hands at her side. Finally, Bram said, "Stop your fidgeting, Ara. Finn said he'd sign on."

Considering Arabella had set up the connection, she knew that. Still, the moment was too important. Before anyone could change their minds, herself included, she wanted her fostering with Lochguard to be a done deal.

The screen filled with Finlay Stewart's cocky grin and some of her agitation eased. Without thinking, she blurted, "You're late."

Finn grinned. "That anxious to talk to me, are you Arabella? Seeing as you're a celebrity now, your fondness is that much more precious."

She opened her mouth to reply when Bram beat her too it. "Stop with the flirting, Stewart. As you can imagine, I have a million things to do. Watching you charm one of my clan members isn't on that list."

Finn replied, "Well, go on, then. What's so urgent it couldn't wait?"

Bram looked up at Arabella and she nodded. Her clan leader looked back to the Scottish leader. "I've decided on the foster for your clan."

Finn's amber gaze flicked up to hers and held it. "Oh, aye?"

Her heart rate kicked up. Finn was looking straight at her, as if he were peering into her very center. For a second, doubts rushed through her mind. Was she really ready to leave Stonefire? Would Lochguard accept her? Would Finn drop his manwhore act once she arrived and ignore her?

And why the bloody hell did his opinion matter? The two of them in a room would kill each other before long.

Bram's voice snapped her back to the present. "Yes, but before I tell you, let me remind you of our earlier discussions. If my clan member is hurt in anyway, I will seriously reconsider our alliance. Understood?"

Finn finally moved his gaze back to Bram. The cockiness was replaced with a hint of anger. "If you think I would intentionally hurt your clan member, then you don't know me at all. Hell, I saved your mate, Bram. I think I deserve a go at your trust."

Bram nodded. "You do, and I appreciated your offer of safe haven on Skye. Still, the clan member going is like a sister to me. I don't want her hurt."

Arabella couldn't take it anymore. "I'm standing right here, Bram. As I told you, I'll be fine."

Finn's eyes met hers and he smiled. "Oh, aye? So you're the one coming." He placed a hand over his heart. "I think my heart just fluttered. I look forward to seeing you again, Arabella. This time, you can't run away."

Arabella stopped breathing. Even though it was through a video feed, she swore Finn's gaze looked determined and a bit hungry.

No. She had to be imagining things. He was wrong for her. Not to mention that while she was making progress on her trauma, she was light-years away from even kissing a male.

Not that she wanted to kiss Finlay Stewart anyway.

Bram growled. "So you'll take Ara?"

Finn smiled. "Of course. I'll have a candidate for you shortly. We can finalize the details when you're not busy watching over your shoulder at every turn. Although I must admit, you've turned into the darling clan of Britain. I'm not sure how I can compete with that."

As Bram and Finn continued to argue like children, all Arabella could think about was how her life would change in two months' time.

Even if it killed her, she would work every day if she had to with Tristan to better know her dragon. She didn't want anyone from Lochguard treating her differently because of an episode. She needed to be stronger, because if she couldn't make a fresh start at Lochguard, Arabella wasn't sure if she'd ever have the chance again.

And if that were the case, she would spend the rest of her life living as a ghost.

CHAPTER TEN

Tapping her fingers against the conference table, Melanie looked yet again at the clock on the wall. The meeting should have started five minutes ago.

The last few weeks had been a blur. Between TV interviews, answering emails, and even holding one video chat with a handful of cabinet officials, Melanie had been busy. When factoring in time with Tristan and their twins, she had barely had enough time to sleep.

Still, she would do it again in a heartbeat because all of that work had brought her to the meeting that should have begun five minutes ago. If the damn woman ever showed up, Mel might be able to enact real change.

Just as she tapped out part of Beethoven's "Ninth Symphony", she heard voices on the other side of the door.

When it opened, Melanie stilled her fingers. It was time.

Standing up, she turned to greet the British Home Secretary, Jacqueline Reid.

A woman in her fifties with graying brown hair and gray eyes smiled as Bram guided her to the table where Melanie waited.

The woman paused and put out a hand. After Mel took it, the woman said, "Thank you for meeting with me, Mrs. Hall-MacLeod."

"The pleasure is mine, Mrs. Reid. And please call me Melanie."

The woman sat across from Melanie. "Since you and I will be talking a lot in the future, call me Jacqueline."

Mel smiled. "Right, then, Jacqueline. I'm glad you were able to come and meet with us. I'd love to chat and share some tea, but we don't have a lot of time. We should start."

Bram was sitting next to Melanie. He jumped in, "I agree. I'm especially keen to hear your response to our proposals."

The Home Secretary looked at each of them in turn. "Before we get to that, I need know if you passed on the necessary information we requested to MI5 or not."

Bram replied, "Yes, they have all of the information we could find on the dragon hunters and the Dragon Knights. Granted, the information on the Dragon Knights is centuries old and may not be much help."

The Home Secretary bobbed her head. "Good. Anything is better than nothing. The public is keen to stop the hunters, thanks to Arabella MacLeod and the other victims. If we don't step up our efforts, we may have a few riots on our hands."

Melanie resisted making a remark about public opinion being more important than the lives of dragon-shifters. It wasn't the time to fight that battle.

Instead, Mel folded her hands in front of her and kept her tone level. "We've fulfilled every request you've asked of us. So, now will you tell us about our proposals?"

"Of course." Jacqueline pulled out some papers from her briefcase and handed one copy each to Melanie and Bram. "There is merit to your ideas, but after talking with the Prime Minister and some other Cabinet ministers, we have some suggested changes."

Revealing the Dragons

Melanie glanced down and read the cover sheet, "Inclusion and Visitation Laws." Looking back up at the Home Secretary, she said, "This stack of paper is at least fifty pages thick. While we'll read through it carefully later, if you could run through the basics for now, we'd much appreciate it."

Jacqueline answered, "The logistics are still being finalized, but visitation passes for humans to enter dragon-shifter territory will be granted on a case-by-case basis, allowing relatives and business interests to visit dragon-shifter land. Nothing is permanent and each case will have a set time period, but no longer will non-sacrifice visits be illegal."

Bram said, "That's a good start. Although, one day, I hope the laws will go further."

Jacqueline tapped her stack of papers. "I understand your desire to do away with the sacrifice system and rule your lands semi-autonomously. However, we're all aware of the growing popularity of the so-called Dragon Knights and their threats. Until we can find a way to contain them, full autonomy, let alone integration, is out of the question or we risk more domestic terrorist attacks."

Before Bram could argue a point he couldn't win, at least not in the present political climate, Melanie stepped in. "That addresses one-half of our proposal. Tell me about the inclusion side of things."

Jaqueline flipped open her papers and tapped on a certain sheet. "Page twenty goes into more detail, but basically, we will allow dragon-shifters more freedom of movement provided they carry a micro-chipped ID card."

Bram crossed his arms. "Storing massive amounts of data on each dragon-shifter in the chips is risky and dangerous. There will be hackers paid to find out our information and pass it on to the highest bidder. We'll become easy targets."

Jacqueline folded her hands on top of her documents. "The ID card is non-negotiable. We will instruct MI5 to do everything in their power to prevent a breach, but too many citizens are scared at the thought of a dragon-shifter running amuck."

Bram shook his head. "I won't allow every secret to be stored by the human government. I can compromise to allow basics or past criminal offenses, but nothing else."

Mel watched as Bram and Jaqueline stared at one another. Bram might look calm and collected on the outside, but Melanie wondered if her leader was as nervous on the inside as she was. If Jacqueline said no, then their hopes of dragon-shifter inclusion would be significantly diminished.

It was the Home Secretary who finally broke the silence. "I'll see what we can do, but even if I can get the Prime Minister to agree, I will need a guarantee that all possible threats are identified. It will only take one rogue dragon terrorizing London to change public opinion and undo all of the progress so far."

Bram answered, "Done. I can't speak for the other clans, but I can assure you that Stonefire will cooperate."

Jacqueline leaned back in her chair. "Yes, well it's a good thing Stonefire is our trial clan. The reputation of some of the other British clans is less than stellar."

Bram added, "Speaking of being the trial clan, I want a guarantee the law on chipped ID cards will be reevaluated on a periodic basis. Maybe every two or three years. And those dragon-shifters who don't visit human populated areas won't be required to carry one."

The Home Secretary nodded. "That sounds reasonable. Although I can't promise anything, I will suggest it. However, these laws will only go into effect in England and Wales. I'm afraid you'll have to talk with the Scottish Parliament and Northern Ireland Assembly to set up laws there."

Sensing Bram was satisfied for the moment, Melanie asked, "How soon will you start issuing visitation passes?"

Jaqueline smiled at her. "You want to see your family."

Mel nodded. "Yes."

"The law will take some time, what with debate and calling a vote, but I've already put in a request for your parents and brother. Provided the Prime Minister doesn't object, you can see them in a few weeks."

Mel swallowed the emotion in her throat. If she wasn't careful, she'd start crying. "Thank you."

Jaqueline waved a hand in dismissal. "Considering the risk you've taken and your determination, it's the least I can do." The Home Secretary placed her documents into her briefcase and looked at both Mel and Bram in turn. "There's little else I can do for the moment. Once you've had a chance to read the proposal thoroughly, contact my office with questions. They'll find you the answers you need."

Jaqueline stood up and Mel hurried to her feet. Since Mel wasn't clan leader, she looked to Bram and he said, "You're welcome back any time, Mrs. Reid. I appreciate you working with us. No one ever gave us a second glance in the past."

Jaqueline shrugged one shoulder. "I've been in politics the majority of my life. I can tell when the wind is changing, and things are definitely changing for the dragon clans in the UK. As long as dragons don't start killing humans at random, I welcome the challenge of devising a new ID system. A person rarely has a chance to make such a mark on history, as I'm sure Melanie is well aware."

After making her goodbyes, the Home Secretary left. When they were alone in the room, Tristan barged in and demanded, "Well?"

Evie was hot on his tail, and moved to stand next to Tristan. She focused her stare on Bram. "Tell us what happened."

Bram raised an eyebrow. "A bit bossy, are you now, lass?"

Evie let out a frustrated sigh. "As much as I like matching wits with you, now is not the time, Bram Moore-Llewellyn. Tell us what the hell happened."

Bram shook his head. "All right, lass. We got most of our demands, but not all."

Tristan looked at Melanie, the unasked question in his eyes. Mel smiled. "We should be seeing my parents and brother soon."

Her mate smiled and walked over to her. Hugging her tightly, he murmured, "I told you we'd find a way, my little human."

Nuzzling his chest with her face, she replied, "I know, but for awhile there, I thought it'd never happen."

Tristan leaned back until he could see her eyes. "But it is, and more, all because of you."

The love and support shining from Tristan's eyes warmed her heart. "Thanks for putting up with me and my sometimes unbearable drive. It's just that if I don't like things as they are, I change them."

Tristan brushed a tendril of hair off her cheek. "Don't ever apologize for being who you are. You've made me a better dragonman, not to mention what you've done for Arabella. I love every bit of your stubbornness, Melanie. Don't ever change."

She tilted her head in invitation, but Tristan looked around the room rather than kiss her. Meeting her eyes again, there was a wicked glint that made her shiver. "Good, they left and even shut the door."

"Why would they—"

"Because, Bram knew I wanted to do this."

Tristan lowered his head and kissed her.

Parting her lips, she accepted his tongue. As he stroked her mouth, she leaned into her mate, loving the feel of his hard body against hers. When Tristan moved one hand to her bum and pressed her against his hard cock, she broke the kiss with a frown. "Tristan MacLeod, we're in the middle of a conference room."

The heat in his eyes shot straight between her legs, making her pussy pulse.

He leaned close, his breath a warm whisper against her cheek. "There aren't any windows or cameras in here. We're safe." He nuzzled her cheek. "I know you want me right now, love. Let's take a chance and celebrate your victory."

While she'd had sex with her mate in a clearing, she'd never had it in such a public area. Yet the idea of maybe being caught sent a little thrill through her body.

What the hell am I thinking?

Before she could think more on the subject, Tristan move his hand from her ass to the hem of her skirt. As he slowly moved up her outer thigh, her breath hitched.

Tristan chuckled. "We're doing this."

She opened her mouth, but then his hand was fingering the seam of her panties. When he growled, the vibrations made her nipples hard.

Her mate murmured, "Why are you wearing underwear? I thought we discussed this before."

"Hey, I'm not about to go commando when meeting the British Home Secretary. Not even for you, Tristan."

He slipped his finger under her panties and thrust it into her pussy. She bit her lip and leaned against his chest for support.

As Tristan slowly moved in and out of her core, it took everything she had to keep from moaning. Somehow she managed to say, "We don't have time for you to tease. Fuck me now, Tristan, or we're leaving."

With a growl, Tristan lifted her, placed her on the table, and spread her legs. The next second, her panties were ripped in half. She barely said, "That's better," when Tristan freed his cock and thrust into her pussy.

Biting her lip harder, Tristan moved, not wasting any time. His actions were hard and fast, in the single-mindedness she'd learned to love. When his eyes flashed to dragon slits and back again, she knew his inner beast was helping him.

Then her mate moved a hand to her clit and circled the hard nub. Placing her hands behind her, Melanie leaned back and widened her legs. Tristan increased his pace and the pressure against her clit. She moaned quietly before whispering, "I'm close."

Pinching her, Melanie's orgasm hit her as wave after wave of pleasure coursed through her body. Tristan never ceased thrusting his hips, and each movement of his cock—as her pussy clenched and released—only increased the pleasure.

Then Tristan stilled and gave a closed-mouth roar as he spilled inside her, sending her into another orgasm.

When she finally came down, Tristan remained inside her as he pulled her close. He kept his voice low. "I think we should add sex in strange places to our bi-weekly date nights."

She was too content to frown. "Something tells me you already have a list a mile long of places for us to try."

"But of course."

His matter-of-fact tone made her smile. "Then maybe I'll think about not wearing any underwear for date nights."

He grunted. "I don't think you should ever wear underwear."

Snuggling into Tristan's chest, she laughed. "Of course you would."

Tristan kissed the top of her head. "Even when you wear underwear, I still love you."

She shook her head against his chest. "You're such a man, Tristan MacLeod."

He leaned back to cup her cheek and stroke her skin with his thumb. "No, love, I'm a dragonman. Get used to it."

Smiling, she looked at her mate with every ounce of love she possessed. "I don't think I'd have it any other way."

As Tristan gave her a slow, gentle kiss, Melanie knew every day would seem like a happy ending as long as she had her dragonman by her side.

Epilogue

Melanie studied the crowd from her vantage point inside the guard's shelter at the main gate to Stonefire. What had once been fifty people had turned into five hundred.

As much as she appreciated the support, the large groups of people showing up every day were making it difficult for anyone to enter the gates and she was expecting some very important guests in the next thirty minutes.

Tristan called out behind her, "Your daughter is awake and wants you."

Mel forced her eyes from the window to Tristan, who was crouched over the playpen.

Annabel made a few baby coos and unintelligible chatter. Mel couldn't resist her daughter's one-sided conversations and walked over to her mate.

Tristan rubbed Mel's back as she leaned over the playpen and smiled at her daughter. "Someone's being chatty." Reaching down, she scooped up her baby girl and settled her on her hip. "But let's try not being too loud or your brother will be cranky. I'd rather your grandparents not have to deal with cranky pants straightaway."

Annabel made a high-pitched squeal and Tristan chuckled. "I don't think Anna wants to be told what to do."

Mel shot her mate a suspicious look. "You're encouraging her when I'm not around, aren't you? She's definitely going to be Daddy's little girl."

Tristan shrugged. "I need someone on my team when she's older. I can't have it always being three against one."

Unable to keep the frown on her face, Melanie laughed. "Oh, I'm working on that. With the twins on my side, we can get rid of that crappy, battered chair in the living room. I swear I'll have to pry your dead body out of it otherwise."

Tristan grinned and the sight warmed Mel's heart. Just as her mate opened his mouth, one of the guards entered from the side door. He looked to Melanie. "A silver sedan is approaching the gate."

Mel whispered, "They're here."

As she moved to the window, her heart beat double-time. She had waited so long for this moment, to see her parents again. She only hoped her memories and dream matched the reality.

She was most afraid of how her brother would treat her. She and Oliver had been close before, but he might see her offering herself as a sacrifice as abandonment.

Tristan moved to her side, a sleepy Jack in his arms. "You video chat with them at least once every two weeks. How can you be nervous?"

She glanced up at Tristan. "You might be oblivious to social awkwardness, since silence is your best friend, but I'm not. Sometimes, video chatting isn't enough."

He frowned. "Stop fretting. I want my practical, logical mate back."

The guard's cell phone beeped. He looked at it and then at Mel and Tristan. "The car is at the gate. Follow me."

They exited the guard's security checkpoint and walked behind the stone and brick building. As they turned the corner, a silver sedan pulled to a stop.

Her heart thumped harder. The doors opened and her parents and brother disembarked the car. They looked around until they met Mel's eyes.

Her mother yelled, "Melanie," before rushing toward them. The next thing she knew, her mother had both her and Annabel in a warm hug.

Her mom whispered, "My baby. I've missed you."

Melanie breathed in the lavender scent of her mother's lotion and a sense of calm came over her. "I've missed you too, Mom."

Mel's mom pulled back and cupped her face. Then she looked to Tristan. "Come here."

Before Tristan could move or say anything, her mom pulled him close into a hug. Mel smiled at the startled expression on her mate's face.

Only when she heard her brother say, "Melanie," did she look away.

Oliver was nearly a foot taller than the last time she'd seen him. While his brown hair and green eyes were the same, his face had lost most of its baby-ness. He even had a faint stubble on his chin. Her little brother was nearly a man.

Before she did something silly, such as cry, Melanie cocked an eyebrow and said, "Is that the way you greet your sister?"

Oliver cocked an eyebrow right back. "I was going to hug you, but now, I'm not sure since giving in to you easily always brings trouble."

She laughed, walked over, and gave her brother a one-armed hug. "I'll keep that in mind."

She peered up and Oliver's eyes glanced to her daughter. He said, "It's still hard to believe I'm an uncle."

Maneuvering Annabel, who merely stared up with big eyes at her uncle, Mel held her out. "Take her. I can already tell she likes you."

Her brother's eyes looked uncertain. "I don't know anything about babies, Mel."

"Pshaw, that doesn't matter." She wiggled Anna a little in the air. "Try it."

Oliver gingerly wrapped Anna in his arms and her daughter smiled and kicked gently against Oliver's stomach.

Mel nodded. "See, I told you, she likes you. Now, if you have the same effect on Jack, I might just have to borrow you once every few weeks."

Oliver gave her a skeptical look. "I'm not sure if I should be afraid or not."

Mel was about to tease her brother some more when their dad walked up. After Mel hugged him, she said, "I hope Mom didn't drive you crazy on the way up."

Her father chuckled. "I've been married to your mom for nearly thirty years. If she were going to drive me mental, she would've done it by now."

Mel's mom shouted, "I heard that, Mr. Hall."

Her dad merely grinned at her mom. Looking back and forth between her parents, a sense of home and belonging came over her. Not even ten years apart would ever change that feeling.

Tristan and her mom joined the little group. Her mom already had Jack in a protective cuddle. She wouldn't be giving up her grandson anytime soon.

Tristan placed a hand on Mel's back and she leaned against him. Her parents glanced at each other. Their looks were filled with love and understanding, as if they were remembering their own first years of marriage.

Oliver, however, focused more on the baby in his arms, probably because he was still unused to the idea of his sister having a husband.

Mel's mother was the one to break the silence. "As much as I love the Lake District, how about we go to your home and have some tea? You two both look exhausted and could use the rest."

Mel rolled her eyes. "You just want time to play with your grandbabies."

"Maybe," her mother simply stated.

Mel's dad shook his head. "Right, then how about we get moving. We only have a week here and I want to make every second count."

Tristan rubbed Mel's back as he answered, "If it's okay with you, James, we'll lead the way."

Mel's dad bobbed his head and Tristan gave Mel a gentle push. She stood her ground and whispered, "Shouldn't we walk beside them?"

Tristan leaned down. "Give them a few minutes to gawk at the dragons overhead. Otherwise, they'll feel obligated to chat with you the whole way."

Mel glanced over her shoulder. Her parents each had a baby in their arms, with Oliver walking between them. As a dragon cried overhead, her brother looked up with fascination.

Turning back around, Melanie harrumphed. "Sometimes you're too perceptive, Tristan MacLeod."

"I'm a teacher, remember? If I didn't pay attention, my classes would devolve into chaos."

The image of ten seven-year-olds running around screaming while Tristan looked on brought a smile to her face. "I somehow doubt that'll happen. One growl would whip them back into shape."

A beat of silence passed before her mate murmured, "You did it, Melanie. Because of you, your parents are here, dragons have a chance at freedom, and our children may have an easier future. You're bloody amazing."

She smiled. "I know."

Tristan barked out a laugh. "So much for modesty."

"I'm just being honest. And you know what? I wouldn't have been able to do any of it without you, Tristan."

Tristan stopped them and turned her face. "We'll always do everything together. No matter what happens, I love you."

"And I love you, Tristan. Now, kiss me."

"In front of your parents?"

"Now you're being modest?"

The corner of his mouth ticked up. "Oh, what the hell."

He moved down to kiss her. Despite the comment from her brother of, "I really don't need to see you kissing anyone, Mel," she leaned into her mate's kiss.

As his tongue stroked hers, Melanie knew that no matter what happened, with the love of her mate, her children, and her family, she could face anything. She wouldn't allow anyone to take away her happily ever after.

Dear Reader:

Thank you for reading Melanie and Tristan's follow-up novella. While they don't have another story out, they do show up in nearly every dragon book I write, so keep a look out! If you enjoyed their story then please consider leaving a review.

Next up is *Healed by the Dragon*, which is about Finlay Stewart and Arabella MacLeod. It takes place on Lochguard and sets up my dragon spinoff series, Lochguard Highland Dragons. While different from Stonefire, I think you'll love the craziness of Lochguard as much as I do!

Turn the page for an excerpt from *Healed by the Dragon*. Thanks for reading!

With Gratitude,
Jessie Donovan

Healed by the Dragon
(Stonefire Dragons #4)

Arabella MacLeod was tortured by dragon hunters a decade ago. Ever since, her clan coddled and tip-toed around her, most especially her older brother. Desperate for a chance at freedom, she volunteers to foster with the Scottish dragon-shifter clan. She's determined to stay clear of the charming Scottish leader, but not only does he keep crossing her path, her dragon is drawn to him.

Finlay Stewart hasn't been able to forget the scarred dragonwoman he met at Stonefire six months ago. When the same female agrees to be fostered with his clan, Finn pursues her. Balancing his clan duties with his need to see Arabella isn't easy, especially with the existing rift in the clan, but he's determined to try. Arabella's inner strength draws him like no other female before.

Will Arabella trust Finn with her past? Or, will the rift in his clan tear them apart?

Excerpt from *Healed by the Dragon*:

CHAPTER ONE

Finlay Stewart eyed his stack of paperwork and resisted the urge to toss it all into the bin. He loved being clan leader of Lochguard far more than he hated it, but there were times when he missed doing things on his own schedule.

His dragon laughed inside his head. *You had better hurry. She will be here in a few hours.*

She's not the reason I want to be done with the bloody paperwork. Our clan needs a new sacrifice.

Believe that if you wish. You can never lie to me.

With a growl, Finn took the next stack of papers and signed line one of about fifty. He wasn't about to be lectured by his bloody dragon.

Aye, Arabella MacLeod was due to arrive in the next few hours to start her trial foster period with his clan. But any clan leader would be anxious at the arrival of someone from a different dragon-shifter clan. Just because Finn enjoyed teasing the lass and riling her up didn't mean everyone else in Lochguard would feel the same, especially given the divide which still ran deep.

His dragon huffed. *You are clan leader. The others will come around.*

It's been nearly a fucking year. I'm impatient and tired of their bullshit.

They will learn.

With a sigh, Finn flipped to the next page of the sacrifice application for the Department of Dragon Affairs. Since the DDA hadn't been accepting applications for the last two months after the attacks in Manchester and London, Finn wanted to be first in line tomorrow when the requests reopened.

Yet as he signed his name for the umpteenth time, his mind wandered to the BBC interview with Arabella MacLeod. No matter how hard he tried, he couldn't forget one sentence she'd said: *A group of men held me down, poured petrol on half of my body, and set me on fire.*

Clenching his pen so hard it snapped, he cursed as ink spilled over his hand. Not wanting to ruin the DDA paperwork, he rushed to the toilet sink. As he washed his hands, he struggled to contain his anger.

The dragon hunters had fucking set Arabella on fire and he wanted to make the bastards pay.

No matter how much he'd argued the point with Bram Moore-Llewellyn, the leader of Clan Stonefire, Bram refused to plan any more attacks on the hunters for the time being. Visitation passes were just starting to be handed out to humans to visit dragon-shifter lands and Bram didn't want to fuck that up.

His dragon spoke up. *He's right. Humans are just starting to reach out to us, and like us. We can't risk ruining our positive image.*

He knew his inner beast was correct, but he didn't like it. *I'm used to how humans in the Highlands treat us. They would never turn us over to the hunters. We've saved their lives too many times in the past.*

His beast didn't disagree, and for good reason; memories were long in the Scottish Highlands.

Still, as he moved back to his desk and attacked his paperwork again, Finn vowed to make Arabella feel safe while she lived with Lochguard. If the dragon hunters thought her easy pickings and came looking, they would have to deal with the wrath of one particular golden dragon.

Finlay Stewart had yet to have any casualties on his own land while in charge. He wasn't about to let that change, not even if a whole fucking army of dragon hunters or the ridiculous Dragon Knights came knocking.

After all, Finn had a few tricks up his sleeve.

His dragon added, *Let them come. I'm bored of always sitting.*

We'll see, dragon. We'll see.

~~~

Arabella MacLeod watched as the Scottish countryside rolled by outside the car window. Deep down, she wished to see all of the crags and peaks from the sky, but despite her best efforts and her brother's help with training, she didn't trust her inner beast enough to shift into her dragon form.

Every time she tried, her nightmares returned.

The inability to shift had nearly cost her the foster position. Only because of her sister-in-law's support was she still going. What Melanie had said to Bram to allow Arabella to go, she had no idea.

Looking to the back seat of the car, her sister-in-law, Melanie, met her eye and smiled. Mel asked, "You nervous yet?"

Arabella's brother, Tristan, grunted from the driver's seat. "Why would you bloody mention that, woman? Now she'll get nervous for sure."

Arabella rolled her eyes at her brother. "Do I look paranoid to you?"

Tristan glanced at her and then back at the road. "You're a MacLeod, which means it's impossible to tell."

She smiled. "MacLeod's are also strong on the inside. If I say I'm fine, I am. I don't need you doubting me now."

Tristan grunted and fell silent. Arabella went back to staring out the car window when Mel said, "If anything happens, anything at all, don't hesitate to call us. I don't care if it's date night or I'm in the middle of a wild dragon-sex marathon, we'll answer for you."

Arabella shuddered. "I don't need images of my brother naked and having sex with anyone."

Mel laughed. "Too bad as he's quite good, you know."

Ara changed the subject. "If I'm in trouble, I'll call. Is that good enough?"

Her brother looked unconvinced, but Melanie answered, "I believe in you, Ara. In six months' time, no one at Lochguard will want to let you go."

Mel's unwavering faith was simultaneously comforting and disconcerting. "We'll see. If my fan group follows me to Scotland, Finn might be begging you to take me back before long."

Melanie laughed. "I think it's cute you have a group who are out to get justice for what was done to you, and will bother any politician who will listen. It won't be long before they have a law named after you to tighten restrictions when it comes to the hunters."

Arabella grunted, not wanting to discuss it further.

Grateful for the silence, Ara memorized the landscape until Tristan turned down the final road leading to Lochguard. Before long, the lake, or loch as they called it in Scotland, came into view. Loch Naver had not only given Lochguard its name, it was also beautiful. The late September sunshine danced on the surface. With the hills and peaks surrounding the long lake, it looked like a picture from a postcard.

REVEALING THE DRAGONS

As the clan's gates appeared in the distance, Arabella rubbed her hand against her trousers as a last-minute panic squeezed her throat.

The first few minutes on Lochguard's land would be critical. She wasn't sure she could handle looks of revulsion or pity. If they all looked at her that way, she may just beg her brother to take her back.

At least, the interview she'd done with the BBC two months ago had allowed everyone to see her face and scars already. It wasn't as if her appearance would be a shock. Or, so she hoped.

Her dragon's voice was low when she spoke. *We will have fun in Scotland. Stop worrying.*

Conversing with her dragon was still difficult for Arabella, but she pushed past her fear. *Thank you.*

Any time. I am always here, Arabella.

I know.

Her dragon backed off and left her alone again.

Arabella let out a sigh. Every adult dragon-shifter spoke of their inner beast as a lifelong friend. She wanted that, too, but after a decade of silence and pushing away her dragon, she wasn't sure if it would ever happen. She might spend the rest of her life with a cautious stranger hovering at the edges of her mind.

Tristan pulled to a stop in front of a set of stone and metal gates. The words, "LOCHGUARD" were spelled out in twining metal above the entrance. Below, in Mersae, the old dragon language, was the phrase, "Love, Loyalty, and Bravery".

Her brother opened his door to exit the car and Melanie followed suit. They waited patiently a few paces off.

Her brother and his mate had been extremely patient and understanding over the last year. The thought of not seeing them for six months brought tears to her eyes.

Stop it, Arabella. It's only six bloody months. You should focus on making new memories. With a deep inhalation, she blinked back the tears and schooled her face into a neutral expression. If she broke down and cried, there was no way her brother would let her out of his sight.

Having a protective older brother was both a blessing and a curse.

Her emotions under control, she opened the door and went over to Melanie and Tristan. She could just make out Melanie saying, "It's rude, Tristan."

Arabella interjected, "What's rude?"

Mel frowned. "You would think someone would greet us at the gate. But no one's here."

Glancing over to the gate, she saw nothing but the stone, metal, and wilderness. She looked back over to Melanie. "We're early."

Melanie opened her mouth just as a familiar Scottish male's voice shouted, "I'm here, I'm here."

The gate opened and Finlay Stewart slowed his pace to a quick walk.

Much like when she'd last seen him in person at Bram's mating ceremony, he was as handsome as ever. Tall, lean, with wind-ruffled blond hair and an ever-present scruff on his face, he was the sort of male who could have any female he wanted.

He was the kind of male who would never want someone like her.

Remembering him flirting with every unmated female back on Stonefire's lands, she managed to get past his attractiveness. Yes, he was fit, but the male was nothing but trouble. She was going to stick to her plan to avoid him. She didn't want his cockiness ruining her first taste of freedom in more than a decade.

Finn approached and Ara schooled her face into borderline boredom. She would be civil, but she wasn't going to let him slip past her barriers like he'd done six months before. Arabella was stronger. Resisting the dragonman should be easier this time around.

———————————

Want to read the rest?
Healed by the Dragon is available in paperback

For exclusive content and updates, sign up for my newsletter at:

http://www.jessiedonovan.com

AUTHOR'S NOTE

I hope you enjoyed this novella. Revisiting former characters is actually extremely difficult for me, but I felt Melanie and Tristan's story wasn't quite done. I think we all now have a better idea of how they work as a couple and how things will be in the future!

As always, I have a lot of people who helped me along the way. I'd like to thank:

- Becky Johnson of Hot Tree Editing. She always pushes me to be better, and I love her for it.
- My betas: Iliana, Donna, and Alyson. They catch the typo or two that slips through the cracks. They also keep me honest, and I'm grateful for that.
- Clarissa Yeo of Yocla Designs. I don't know what I'll ever do if she stops making covers!
- My readers and fans. You all make this worth it!

Thanks again for reading and I can't wait to share Finn and Arabella's story in *Healed by the Dragon*. I hope you continue to follow the stories of Clan Stonefire (and Clan Lochguard).

See you around! :)

ABOUT THE AUTHOR

Jessie Donovan wrote her first story at age five, and after discovering *The Dragonriders of Pern* series by Anne McCaffrey in junior high, she realized people actually wanted to read stories like those floating around inside her head. From there on out, she was determined to tap into her over-active imagination and write a book someday.

After living abroad for five years and earning degrees in Japanese, Anthropology, and Secondary Education, she buckled down and finally wrote her first full-length book. While that story will never see the light of day, it laid the world-building groundwork of what would become her debut paranormal romance, *Blaze of Secrets*. In late 2014, she officially became a *New York Times* and *USA Today* bestselling author.

Jessie loves to interact with readers, and when not traipsing around some foreign country on a shoestring, can often be found on Facebook. Check out her page below:

http://www.facebook.com/JessieDonovanAuthor

And don't forget to sign-up for her newsletter to receive sneak peeks and inside information. You can sign-up on her website:

http:///www.jessiedonovan.com

CPSIA information can be obtained
at www.ICGtesting.com
Printed in the USA
LVOW08s1503271216
518827LV00002B/244/P